THE HEIR

A CURVY GIRL MC ROMANCE

NICHOLE ROSE

CONTENTS

Dedication

To the family who chooses us.

About the Book

Can a billionaire biker and his rival's curvy little sister find forever together...or is blood really thicker than water?

Andreas Romano

Thanks to my father's shady business practices, my life has devolved into putting out one fire after another.

The latest? Dealing with the rival MC he hired to strong-arm federal regulators into looking the other way.

The Hell's Vipers have been nothing but trouble.

Until I stumble across Catriona Grady, their VPs curvy little sister.

Her bright eyes and sweet smile are pure sunshine.

But falling for her promises nothing but trouble for me and my MC.

I guess it's a good thing I've never been one to run from a fight.

Because this little light is mine.

Catriona Grady

People always say blood is thicker than water, but they forget the rest of that saying.

My older brother may have raised me, but he's been nothing but trouble.

He treats me like property, and I'm not interested in being owned.

Until I run into his enemy, Andreas Romano.

When Andreas touches me, I come undone.

I'm falling hard for the gorgeous billionaire.

But there's no way my brother will let him have me without a fight.

It's time to choose my side.

Family...or forever?

CHAPTER ONE
Andreas

"I don't want to move back to Silver Spoon Falls," Autumn complains, throwing her hands up in the air and scowling at me. With her dark hair up in a bun and stilettos on, she looks ready for war as she paces across my expansive office. "Good grief, Andreas. What do you not get about that?"

"It's one year, baby sister," I say, trying not to push too hard. That never works with Autumn. She's as stubborn as she is skittish. As soon as she feels cornered, she bolts. Like so much else, I blame our father for that. Vincent Romano had a vision for her life and didn't much care whether hers matched or not.

She ran as soon as she turned eighteen and hasn't set foot in Silver Spoon Falls since. I barely got her back for the old bastard's funeral last year. Trying to convince her to move back has been an exercise in futility. But I miss the hell out of her. And I want her where I can keep an eye on her.

My sister is complicated. She has a heart bigger than this state, a mouth that never stops, and a penchant for thinking she can singlehandedly save the world. More often than not, she makes waves that land her in hot water.

Her latest issue is proof of that. She and our father's former business partner, Jimmy Gatlin, got into a heated argument at the airport the day she flew in. Ordinarily, that wouldn't have been a big deal, but Autumn doesn't mince words, and someone caught the whole thing on camera. Now, the entirety of the internet is calling him Short Dick Man.

They're crucifying him, and he's out for blood.

Jimmy's a crooked motherfucker who should have been in prison a long time ago. The best thing my father ever did was cut ties with him the day he sent Autumn a picture of his cock when she was sixteen. But he's threatening to sue her for defamation and slander. And I don't have time to juggle one more thing right now.

I'm already up to my eyes in problems. My father was not a good man. He was an even worse businessman. He nearly ran our shipping company, Romano International, into the ground by making shitty business decisions and backdoor deals. The illegal dumping was the worst. God only knows how many gallons of hazardous chemicals he pumped into the oceans.

Before his untimely demise, he hid his crimes by hiring a shady lawyer. Said lawyer's solution to dealing with federal regulators was hiring the Hell's Vipers, an outlaw MC, to strong-arm them into looking the other way. They did a lot of other dirty shit for my father too.

By the time all was said and done, Montoya Investments, Jason "Cash" Montoya's grandfather's company was embroiled in the mess, nearly destroying both companies. Cash, the President of our MC, and I have been picking up the pieces ever since. Romano International and Montoya Investments are slowly recovering under our leadership. But it's been a goddamn nightmare for both of us.

Case in point: the Hell's Vipers. One of the first things we did when we found out about my father's arrangement with them was to end it. No more shady deals, no more dirty deeds...no more money changing hands. They're pissed about it.

A couple months ago, they came after Cash's wife, Hadley. Except they're fucking morons. Hadley has a twin sister. I'm guessing whoever the Vipers sent didn't know that though. They picked the wrong twin, thinking they got Cash's wife. Kyra ended up with some bumps and bruises, but was otherwise okay, thank God.

We rallied the troops and tightened security, ready for whatever bullshit they decided to pull next...only for them to go strangely quiet. Ordinarily, this would be a good thing, but I'm not convinced it is. As we recently learned, the Hell's Vipers are in bed with the Satan's Savages, the outlaw MC who murdered Tate "Hands" Grimes's sister-in-law and nearly killed an innocent baby. Had Tate's sister-in-law not managed to get her baby out, the little girl would have died.

I don't like that the Savages are connected to the Vipers. I don't like that the Vipers have been so quiet. Quite frankly, I don't fucking like any of it. Period. I know the police and feds are working to bring the Savages and the Vipers down, but until they do, there's nothing stopping the Vipers from coming for us. Silence isn't always golden. Sometimes, it's a precursor to the storm.

And that's what fucking worries me.

They're up to something. I'd very much like to know what.

"Look," Autumn huffs. "It's not like I knew anyone was filming. And he's the one who called me a stuck-up bitch first." She scowls at nothing, her cocoa-colored eyes snapping fire. "As if I owe him common courtesy after he sent me that dick pic and scarred me for life. The man is delusional!"

"He is delusional," I agree, clenching my hands into fists beneath the desk at the reminder of the picture Jimmy sent her. I still want to kill the motherfucker for that. He's lucky I was working on my MBA out of state when it happened. They'd still be fishing pieces of him out of the Gulf if I had been here.

Instead, my father took everything and left him bankrupt. I'm not sure if he did it for Autumn or if he simply used the situation to squeeze Jimmy out, but I don't tell her that. She deserves at least one decent memory of the man who raised us. God knows, there aren't many of those.

Which is the other reason I want her back here. Silver Spoon Falls always felt more like a prison to my sister than a home. It's full of bad memories she's been running from for far too long. I don't want her to spend the rest of her life trying to outrun our father's ghost. It's time for her to come home and put him to rest once and for all. She'll never be truly happy until she does.

"I'll make you a deal," I say, watching her over my massive desk. Like usual, it's covered in stacks of paperwork. It's going to take a decade to go through it all, but I'm meticulously working my way through every record we have, trying to restore the company to what it should have been all along. That's going to take years too.

I've been able to keep most of my father's misdeeds from being made public, but I'm certainly not fucking doing it to protect his memory. That's tarnished beyond repair. My only concern is the thousands of people who work for me. Romano International is multi-national. We have offices in eight different nations with thousands of employees to protect. I won't allow them to suffer because of what my father did. He put them through enough when he was alive.

"What deal?" Autumn eyes me suspiciously, her arms crossed, and lips pursed like she thinks I'm up to something. I see the curiosity in her eyes though. My baby sister can't resist a good negotiation, especially if it means getting something she wants. She rarely asks for much.

"If you'll agree to come home for one year, I'll let you rewrite our environmental protection policies," I say. Her degree is in environmental science. It's her passion. Before our father died, it was the biggest source of contention between them. She hated that he flouted the rules so flagrantly. He hated that she did everything she could to make him pay the price. She's been arrested twice for protesting company policies.

"You're serious," she says after a minute.

"Have I ever lied to you?"

"Um, yes!" she cries. "You told me that spiders are more scared of me than I am of them, which is so not true. And then you told me that the guy at the haunted house wasn't going to chase me with a chainsaw. I nearly died, by the way. And let's not forget the time you told me that Smokey ran away."

I grimace. "I forgot about Smokey."

"I didn't," she sniffs. "Goldfish don't even have legs, Andreas."

"I panicked," I say with a shrug. "I thought it was better than telling you the cat ate him."

Her eyes grow wide with horror. "Tobias *ate* him?"

"Shit," I mutter, raking a hand through my hair. I forgot she didn't know that part.

"All this time I thought you accidentally flushed him down the toilet or he jumped out of the bowl or something," she says with a shudder. "Instead, your cat was a murderer."

I decide not to remind her that Tobias was her cat. Call me crazy, but I don't think it'll win me any points here. I'm already skating on thin ice with her. If I push much harder, she'll be on the first flight back to California.

"My point," I say instead, trying to get us back on track before I manage to taint more of her childhood memories or push her out the door, "is that I finally have a chance to run this company the right way. But I need your help to do it. Give me one year, and you can write whatever policies you want to write when it comes to environmental protection. No matter what it costs, I'll make sure we implement and follow them."

"You've always loved this company," she says.

I shrug instead of trying to explain. To her, this company is just an extension of our father. To me, it's an opportunity to leave behind something better. He never cared about the people or the culture. He never cared about family. Everything was about power and influence to him. His shadow still clings to this company, just like it does to our family. I want to erase it. It's the least I owe our employees after the decades of loyalty they showed a man who didn't deserve it.

"One year?" Autumn asks.

"Three-hundred and sixty-five days."

"Do I have to live with you?"

"You can have the estate if you'd rather," I offer, knowing there's not a chance in hell she'll take me up on that. She hasn't stepped foot in our childhood home since she left it. But I don't want her on her own right now. Not with the Vipers out there. Not with Jimmy Gatlin out for blood.

"No thanks," she says, wrinkling her nose in distaste. "I'll stay at your place."

I fight a smile. She acts like my place is a one-bedroom studio with no privacy instead of an eight-thousand square foot mansion with a guest wing. Hell, I think she'd prefer the one-bedroom studio. Money never mattered much to Autumn. She always had plenty of that. It was freedom she craved. After our mom died when she was fourteen, she didn't have much of that.

I wish like hell I'd known then how bad things were for her. I would have dropped everything and come home. She wouldn't have had to face it alone. But she never said a word until the day she left home. She didn't want me to know.

"You aren't allowed to pay me a ridiculous salary," she says. "Or give me a fancy title. I don't want people thinking this is permanent."

"I think I can arrange that," I say, relaxing slightly.

She expels a long-suffering sigh, looking at me like she's headed toward the gallows instead of moving home for a year. "Fine. Then I guess I'll move here for a year." She throws up a hand. "But only for a year. And only because it'll be good for the environment."

"Noted," I say, fighting a smile. She's coming home. Fucking finally.

"Your sister is hot," Cormac "Giant" Carmichael says, grinning at me over my desk an hour later. He props one boot on the edge, leaning back in his chair with his hands laced together behind his head, the picture of casual comfort.

He came in as she was headed out. They haven't met before now. I don't think Autumn knew what to think of him. He's big, loud, and has never met a stranger in his life. She's hesitant about the MC in general. Like most people, she doesn't know much about MCs like ours. It's a whole new world to her. But she'll get used to my brothers.

"I will kill you," I say, staring at Giant levelly. He thinks he's funny, but he's not. He plays too fucking much. Besides, he and Autumn would never work. Ever. Autumn needs someone who won't smother her. She grew up watching our father cage our mother and call it love. She needs someone who can protect her without going overboard. That isn't Giant. Everything he does is overboard. When he falls, he's going to be an overprotective son of a bitch. It's in his blood.

His grin widens.

"I'm serious, Cormac," I growl. "I will kill you."

"Damn, brother," he says, laughing loudly. "Make a motherfucker feel special, why don't you?"

I shake my head at him. "Is there a reason you're in my office bugging me?"

"Uh, yeah." He makes a show of looking around my office. "Your office is a helluva lot nicer than mine."

He's full of shit. I mean, yeah, my office is nice. Three walls are all glass, looking out over Silver Spoon Falls and the harbor. The late afternoon sun spills through the windows, glinting off the hardwood floor. Despite the paperwork stacked everywhere, there's enough space in here to keep it from being cramped or cluttered. It's relaxing, peaceful.

But his office isn't anything to sneeze at either. It's state of the art, with security features most people only dream about. But Giant wasn't made to sit behind a desk. It drives him up the fucking wall. I'm pretty sure the man has ADHD. He never stays in one place for long, is always doing fifteen things at once, and couldn't sit still if his life depended on it. The only time he's ever chill is when he's on the back of his bike.

"I'm bored out of my fucking mind," he says right on cue, picking up a paperweight from my desk and tossing it into the air. "So I was thinking."

"Lord help us all," I mutter drily.

"Man, fuck you," he says, laughing. "You wish you had this brain."

"I wouldn't wish that brain on anyone."

He stops tossing the paperweight to flip me off. "Whatever. My brain is sexy, and you know it. But my fucking point was that I'm not doing anything and you're not doing anything."

I spread my hands out to indicate my desk and the stack of shit I'm very clearly doing.

He ignores me, of course. "So we might as well go do some recon."

Well, now he has my interest. "What kind of recon?"

"The kind that involves finding out what the fuck the Vipers are doing," he says. "Don't tell me you aren't curious as a motherfucker why they haven't made a move since Kyra. They're up to something. I feel it in my gut."

"Fuck. You too?"

He nods. "It's too goddamn quiet. That's never a good sign. Either they're up to something or they've moved on to someone else. Either way, I'd like to know once and for all if we can ease off on security or if we need to keep stressing about this shit. My goddamn ball hairs are going gray."

"You do know there is some shit I don't need to hear, right?" I ask.

He shrugs one massive shoulder, tossing my paper-weight into the air again. "You probably prune yours into hearts or some shit like that." A sly grin spreads across his face. "Do you get your arsehole steamed too?"

"You spend too much fucking time with models," I say, shaking my head. Only they would think up some bullshit like getting your asshole steamed.

His grin widens. "You're the only model I know."

"I'm not a goddamn model," I growl, flipping him off this time.

My face has been splashed across more magazine covers than I can count. I've been on every Most Eligible list in the country since I was twenty-one. My brothers gave me the nickname *Playboy* as a result. They think that shit is hilarious and give me nine kinds of hell about it.

I know what I look like and what people say about me. But they don't know me. Those who do, like Giant, know what I'm really about. They know who I really am. They may give me shit, but they know I'm not a fucking model, I'm not a pretty boy, and I'm not interested in living the high life or any of that bullshit. I've got bigger fish to fry and more important shit to do.

"He doth protest too much," Giant says.

"Asshole," I laugh, chunking a pen across the desk at him.

He bats it away with the back of his hand, sending it flying across the room. He doesn't even miss a beat catching the paperweight as it descends from the air.

"Have you heard anything else about the case on the Savages?" I ask.

He shakes his head, scowling. "Cops aren't telling me or Fifth shit," he says, referring to Jude Despora, our club's lawyer. "All we know is they've got someone deep undercover and they're trying to keep from blowing his cover before he gets the intel he needs to secure the case. It could be days. It could be weeks. I guess it depends on how dirty the Savages really are."

"Fuck," I growl, wishing they'd hurry the hell up and get on with it. Cash is worried as fuck about the Vipers coming after Hadley, who is pregnant. Landon "Cowboy" Rickman is losing his mind worrying about them coming after Kyra again. Hands has his hands full taking care of Scout, the baby girl the Savages nearly killed. They're all doing a good job holding it together, but I know them, and I know it hasn't been as easy as they make it look.

They're worried, and they'll continue to worry until the Vipers and the Savages are dealt with. I can't do anything about the Savages. That situation is out of my hands. But my father is the reason we're in the shit with the Vipers. Until the feds handle them, I owe it to my brothers to find out what they fuck they're planning and put a stop to it.

The paperwork will still be here tomorrow.

"Let's ride," I say to Giant, my mind made up.

Chapter Two

Catriona

"You have got to be kidding me," I mumble, gaping as two giants slip down the alley behind my brother's pawnshop as I walk toward my car after closing up. They're pretty sneaky for giants, I'll give them that. Had I not been watching the shadows so closely I wouldn't have noticed them at all. But my older brother, Connor, attracts the worst kind of trouble.

I learned a long time ago to keep my eyes peeled. I refuse to end up a statistic, kidnapped and murdered before I even reach my twentieth birthday.

I pause in the middle of the sidewalk, looking around. The street is deserted. In Copper Creek, it usually is once the sun goes down. Unlike Silver Spoon Falls, the thriving community a short drive away, business isn't booming in Copper Creek. The small town has been slowly dying since I was a little girl. The only people left are those in no hurry to get out...the old-timers, the lifers, and the troublemakers.

And, apparently, the two goons breaking into my brother's pawnshop.

I briefly consider letting them do it and then sigh. Connor will lose his mind. War will be declared. Vengeance will be sought. Blood will be shed. And I'll end up spending even more of my life checking every shadow.

Connor will also lose his mind if I call the cops. He has a history with them, none of it good. It comes with the territory when you're VP of an outlaw MC. God only knows how much of the crap he pawns inside the shop is stolen. It's why he adamantly refuses to let me do anything more than clean up the place and answer the phones. I don't argue with him. The less I know, the better.

I love Connor, really I do. When our parents died in a car accident when I was twelve, he raised me. He was barely twenty-one, working in the oilfields just trying to keep us together. He was normal. And then he met Rooster and joined the Hell's Vipers.

Nothing has been the same since. *Connor* hasn't been the same since. I used to dream about getting us both out of this town. Now, well, now I'm not so sure I'll ever get him out of here. This life didn't choose him. He chose it. I spend half of my time trying to keep him out of prison, and the other half feeling guilty for wanting to get myself out of here in one piece.

It looks like tonight is going to be more of option one.

"If I get kidnapped or die tonight, I'm coming back to haunt you," I mutter and then adjust my car keys, holding them like a weapon. They probably won't do me much good, but they're better than nothing. I take a breath and hurry across the street, my heart beating so fast I'm a little afraid I'm going to have a freaking heart attack and die on the sidewalk.

I was not made for confrontation or acts of bravery. I'm much more suited to reading about them from the safety of my bedroom. But I've gotten good at faking it until I make it. I can cry later.

I work up what little nerve I possess and poke my head into the dark alley.

"Excuse me?" I call, proud when my voice doesn't waver. "If you're trying to break in, you should probably reconsider. My brother owns the place, and we have cameras. He's pretty good at hunting down people who cross him.

Fencing stolen jewelry for a few bucks isn't worth what he'll put you through when he finds you."

"What the fuck?" one of the men growls. His voice is rich and smooth like expensive whiskey, and I immediately like it.

"Who says we're breaking in?" the other asks, his tone full of amusement.

"You're creeping around an alley after dark." Once the light trickling in from the street ends a few feet in, there's nothing but inky blackness in the alley. There isn't even moonlight to help illuminate the way.

"I had to take a leak," the amused one says.

"And you needed your friend to hold it for you?" I snark.

"Sweetheart, you couldn't pay me enough to let that bastard near my cock," the amused one drawls. "It'd break his wee little heart to see it."

There. He's to the left.

I turn in that direction and squint. A thick shadow—more solid than the rest—moves at the far end of the alley, near the back door of the pawnshop. The would-be burglar is far enough away that I relax slightly. He hasn't tried to come any closer.

Where's the other one?

"Aww, would he feel bad for you?" I ask, sarcasm heavy in my voice. "You know, it's okay if you're a grower and not a show-er. Even though you all claim you're walking around with anacondas in your pants, most men are."

The amused one barks laughter. "You're a ballsy little thing, aren't you?"

"Who says I'm little?"

"Is she little, Playboy?"

"Tiny," the other one says from behind me, his voice whisper soft.

I open my mouth to scream, but it's already too late. The man grabs me before I can make a sound, gently clamping his hand over my mouth. Stupidly, I forget about the keys in my hand until they hit the ground at my feet. Panic seizes me, and I just...let them go.

"Easy, little one," he murmurs, his voice a velvety rasp of sound in my ear as he hauls me up against his body. "Easy. I'm not going to hurt you."

Right. I bet that's what all kidnappy murderers say right before they throw you into the back of a Chester the Molester van. Then you disappear, only to turn up unalive in the middle of the desert ten years later.

This one doesn't sound like a kidnappy murderer, though. He doesn't feel like one either. Are they all this hard? And dressed in fancy suits? Better question...why is a guy in a fancy suit trying to break into my brother's pawnshop?

And why does he smell so good?

"Mmphmm mmph mmmph mmm!"

"What'd she say?" the amused one asks, jogging up to us.

"How the fuck should I know?" Fancy Suit asks, holding me pressed tight against his body. He keeps me subdued but does it carefully as if he's trying not to hurt me. Interesting behavior for a kidnapper.

"She's probably insulting your cock," the amused one says.

"Mmmph mmm mmph," I mutter, trying to tell them that they're both idiots.

"I have no idea what you're saying, little one," Fancy Suit says and sighs. "We're not breaking into the pawnshop, and we're not trying to hurt you. If I let you go, don't scream. That'll just piss me off."

"All work and no fun makes Playboy a grumpy mother-fucker," the amused one says.

Playboy. That's the second time he's called him that. Is it a road name? There's no way these two are in the Vipers. I haven't even gotten a good look at them, and I already know neither fits the bill. They're too...different. Playboy is wearing a suit, for one. I doubt a single brother in the Vipers even owns a suit. And the other one is funny. None of the Vipers possess that particular trait. Plus, they wouldn't be sneaking around the pawnshop if they were my brother's friends.

"Shut the fuck up, Giant," Playboy growls at his friend.

Giant chuckles, unoffended.

"Don't scream," Playboy says, his voice at my ear. He hesitates and then slowly pulls his hand away from my mouth.

I briefly think about screaming just because he told me not to do it, but then decide against it. I might be crazy—I'm pretty sure I *am* crazy—but I actually believe him. I don't think he wants to hurt me.

"Why are you sneaking around my brother's pawnshop?" I ask.

"Your brother is Connor Grady?"

"I didn't say that," I lie.

"Right," Giant chuckles. He looms into view suddenly. And whoa. He's even more massive than I thought he was. He reminds me of a cage fighter, only with a little boy smile, dimples, and pure wickedness in his gray eyes. "He's the owner of this here fine establishment."

"Which makes you Catriona Grady," Playboy says.

I shiver at the sound of my name on his lips. It sounds beautiful...seductive.

"Will you let me go?" I growl at him, wiggling in his hold.

"Hell no," he rasps. "I like you right where you are, little one."

"Stop calling me that."

"You are little," Giant says.

"Only because you grew up with Goliath and his friends up the beanstalk," I mutter, still struggling in Playboy's arms. I may be short, but I'm far from small. I wear a size twenty-two on a good day. I've got more boobs and more butt than I know what to do with. Usually, I hide them in oversized hoodies. It keeps Connor from flipping out when his creepy friends leer at me. As if it's my fault they think anything with a vagina is fair game.

"She's mouthy," Giant chuckles.

Playboy sighs, his warm breath ruffling pieces of my blonde hair. It blows across the side of my face, sending another shiver through me. My stomach quivers and trembles, though I don't know why. There's no way I'm attracted to this man. I don't even know what he looks like!

He feels good, though, a little voice whispers. It's not wrong. It's been a long time since anyone held me. I can't even remember when anyone other than Connor hugged me. I'm not even sure I remember the last time *he* hugged me. This feels a little too much like a hug.

"If you aren't here to hurt me, can you please let me go?" I plead quietly.

Playboy must hear the quiver in my voice because he immediately releases me. I stumble a step before I manage to catch myself. As soon as I'm steady, he spins me around to face him. The instant I catch sight of him, I realize two things simultaneously.

I know this man.

And I'm in far more danger than I thought.

Playboy, or Andreas Romano, is a member of the Silver Spoon MC. He's also a billionaire. His picture has graced the front of every business magazine in the country, most of the fashion and society magazines too. He's freaking gorgeous. And I don't mean in the carefully coiffed way most of the upper echelon of society are gorgeous. I mean he's five-alarm fire gorgeous.

I read somewhere that his mom was Greek, and his father was Italian. It shows. His dark hair is wild on top but faded on the sides, making him look both put together and a little bit wild at the same time. His onyx bedroom eyes hide behind a prominent brow and long lashes. His full lips and sharp jawline are literal freaking perfection. His olive skin has a healthy, natural glow even in the semi-darkness.

He's not quite as big as his friend, but he towers over me, eclipsing me. I feel small in his presence, vulnerable. It's strange though. Even knowing who he is, I don't feel like I'm in danger. In fact, as he stares at me with his eyes an inexplicable mix of hard and soft, I feel...safer than I have in a long time.

What the hell?

"You didn't scream," he says, watching me intently.

"You told me not to."

Giant chuckles like he finds this funny.

Andreas shifts his gaze from me to him. "Go keep an eye out," he says.

"You're ruining my fun."

"Dodging a hail of bullets if the Vipers catch us snooping around will ruin more than your fun," Andreas says, his eyes on me again.

"Good point." Giant peers down at me. "See ya around, Bad Ass."

He ducks out of the alley before I can say anything, leaving me alone with Andreas. I gulp and take a step backward, putting a little distance between me and my brother's enemy. I don't know much about the Silver Spoon MC or what happened between them, but I do know whatever they did has had the Vipers stomping around for months, swearing vengeance. And I know Andreas's company is at the heart of whatever happened.

I also know his father, Vincent Romano, was a foul human being. Before he died, he came here a few times to meet with my brother and Rooster. He acted like he was at risk of catching the plague the entire time, sneering down his nose at everyone and everything. I disliked him on sight.

"You know who I am, don't you?" Andreas asks me.

"Andreas Romano," I say and then bite my lip. Maybe I should have lied to him.

"It's all right," he says. "I'm not going to hurt you."

"You keep saying that."

"You keep looking at me like you're waiting for me to kidnap you."

"The thought crossed my mind."

Something like annoyance flashes in his eyes, his lips compressing into a hard line. "Not all MCs are like your brother's, Catriona."

"Says the man sneaking around his pawnshop," I snort.

"We were just doing a little recon," he says, holding up his hands. I remember what they felt like against me and my belly quivers again.

"Recon for what?"

"Are you one of their sweet butts, little one?"

"Am I one of their...?" I trail off, gaping at him. Oh, the nerve of this man! "First of all, buddy," I growl, poking him in the chest. "That's disgusting. You couldn't pay me enough to sleep with them. Second of all, you have a lot of nerve being all judgy and nosy when you're the one creeping around doing criminal things. Third of all, it's rude to answer a question with a question. And fourth..." I splutter, trying to think of something else to add, but all I can come up with is, "go kick rocks, you big jerk!"

"It was just a question, Catriona," he murmurs, a ghost of a smile touching his full lips. Of course he's amused. Jerk. "I didn't intend to offend you."

"Well, you did," I sniff. "You might be a manwhore, but that doesn't give you the right to assume that I'm a lady-whore."

"A manwhore? I'm definitely not that."

"Whatever. Can you please leave now?"

"No."

I blink at him. "No?"

"No."

"What do you mean no?"

"I'm not a manwhore," he says, ignoring my question. "I don't sleep around."

Oh my gosh. He's insane.

"I don't care!" I cry, throwing my hands up in the air. "I just want you to leave before my brother gets here and finds you." I think I might be lying though. A tiny part of me is...relieved this man isn't like my brother and his friends. Which makes no sense to me. What does it matter if he sleeps around or not? Why should I care? He's nothing to me but a temporary inconvenience.

Liar, a little voice whispers.

I really wish it'd stop doing that.

"Did you know the Vipers attacked one of our women a couple months ago?" Andreas asks suddenly.

I blink rapidly, caught off guard by his question. "You're lying."

"Ask your brother if you don't believe me," Andreas says, sympathy in his voice, as if he feels badly for being the one to shatter my illusions about Connor. I don't have many left when it comes to my brother, but that one....

"Connor wouldn't do that."

"The Vipers roughed her up in her flower shop." Andreas leans back against the wall behind him, oblivious to how dirty the alley is or how much it's going to cost to get the dirt and grime off his suit. "He's the VP. Whether he was there in person or not, you know as well as I do that he was involved in the decision to carry out the attack on her."

I lick my lips, not sure if he's telling me the truth or if he's trying to manipulate me for some reason. Surely it's the latter. Connor may be a lot of things, but he's not that far gone. Not yet. There's still good inside him. I know it. He wouldn't order an attack on an innocent woman, would he?

Uncertainty creeps through me.

"Why are you telling me this?" I demand.

Andreas hesitates for a moment, almost like he isn't sure why he's telling me this himself, and then he curses. "Because I know what it's like to live with someone who does whatever the fuck they want regardless of who it hurts," he says. "You need to leave, little one. If you don't, he's going to drag you down with him. He's in trouble. Big trouble. You don't want to be collateral damage."

"What are you talking about?" I demand, gaping at him. "What do you mean he's in trouble? What are you guys going to do to them?"

"Us?" He gives his head a short, frustrated shake. "I told you already. We aren't like the Vipers, little one. We aren't outlaws. My MC wants nothing to do with any of that bullshit. I'm only here to figure out what your brother and his friends are going to throw at us next. We're trying to protect our people, that's it."

"Then why do you think he's in trouble?"

Andreas sighs. "It's a long fucking story."

"Tell it fast."

"Here," he says instead, reaching into his pocket. I jump back a step, ready to make a run for it, only to blush when he pulls out a small square of paper and passes it to me. He notices my reaction, but he doesn't comment on it. "This is my address. Ask him about the girl and then come find me. I'll tell you anything you want to know." He hesitates, his black gaze shifting over my face. "Just make sure you're ready to hear it."

"You want me to spy on him," I spit, glancing at the business card he handed me.

"No," he growls, grabbing my wrist before I can storm off. His eyes blaze with holy fire. "I want to kiss those eyes soft and then put your infuriating little ass on the back on my bike and get you the hell out of here. But I'm walking away now and hoping like hell you come to me when you're ready to talk. You need me, little one. I'll wait however long I have to wait for you to realize it too."

"I..."

He cuts me off with his lips against mine, his kiss as thrilling as it is surprising. His hand sinks into my hair, angling my head. His lips are soft, his kiss curiously gentle. I soften beneath him without meaning to, my entire body going pliant in his arms. He steals my breath and every thought in my head, leaving my mind silent and my body aching, yearning for something I'm not even sure I understand. His tongue touches my bottom lip, a low growl vibrating from his chest.

My entire *soul* quivers at the sound, something inside bubbling up swiftly in response.

It's over as quickly as it began. He makes a sound that's a mix between agony and bliss, and then sets me away from him, his rough hands gentle. I sway on my feet, reaching out to grasp the wall for support.

"Ask him, Catriona," he says, already headed toward the mouth of the alley. "And then come to me. I can help you. You just have to let me. Don't let him find my card."

I curl my fist around it, hiding it in my palm.

Andreas disappears around the corner, leaving my mind reeling.

What in the hell is going on?

"You're actin' weird," Connor says, narrowing his eyes on me across the dinner table. "What's up with you?"

"Nothing," I mutter, dropping my gaze to my plate. I've barely touched it. My mind has been running in circles ever since I stumbled across Andreas and Giant a week ago. I'm not sure what to make of anything Andreas said, but my gut tells me that he wasn't lying to me. Which is exactly why I haven't brought it up to Connor.

I'm a little afraid of what happens when I do. Will he even tell me the truth? He rarely does when it comes to the MC. He tries to keep me out of it as much as possible. He says he doesn't want that side of his life to touch me. Ironic considering that it's seeped into every aspect of *my* life over the last few years.

The MC is everywhere, polluting everything. Half the time, I can't even escape them in my own home because they're here, lounging around like they own the place. The only time I get to myself is when I lock myself in my room, put on my headphones, and get lost in a book. They don't follow me into the fictional worlds I travel into. I spend a lot of time reading as a result.

"You're a shit liar, baby sister," Connor says. "You on the rag again or somethin'?"

"Jesus, Connor," I say, rolling my eyes. "I know it's hard for your pea brain to comprehend this but try to keep up for once, okay? Not every emotion a woman has is tied to her menstrual cycle."

"Watch your smart mouth," he growls.

I roll my eyes at him again. I'm not afraid of him. He may be gruff and crude and a million other things, but he's never raised a hand against me. Honestly, he treats me like I'm untouchable most of the time. He's annoyingly overprotective. It drives me crazy.

I can go anywhere I want in this town and do anything I want in this town. No one really bothers me because they're afraid of him. The only problem is that there is nothing to do here. Every dream I have involves getting out of Copper Creek. And that's the one thing he won't let me do. He wants me right where I am so he can keep an eye on me. He says it's for my safety.

In his eyes, I'm sure it is. But I feel like I'm living in a prison.

"I'll watch my mouth if you stop being misogynistic."

"There you go with that shit again," he mutters, taking a drink of his beer.

"If the shoe fits," I say, batting my lashes at him.

"I love women," he protests.

I hesitate for a long moment, my stomach churning. "Is that why you ordered the Vipers to attack one a few months ago?" I finally ask, my voice soft.

He pauses with his beer halfway to his mouth. "Who the fuck told you that?"

"Were they lying?"

"Who told you, Catriona?"

My heart sinks all the way into my soles. Andreas wasn't lying. They really did attack an innocent woman, and Connor knew it. He was involved. Anger and disappointment swell in my chest, tears stinging my eyes.

"Connor," I whisper.

"Don't say my name like that," he says, setting his beer down on the table. He avoids my gaze, his jaw clenched. "This doesn't concern you, Catriona. Tell me who told you so I can handle the problem."

"You guys attacked an innocent woman and all you have to say for yourself is that it doesn't concern me?" I gape at him. "Are you freaking kidding me right now? God, Connor, listen to yourself! What is wrong with you?"

"Nothing," he snaps. "There's nothing wrong with me."

"There is if you think any of this is okay," I snap right back at him, jumping to my feet. "Good grief. What *happened* to you? You aren't even someone I recognize anymore. You definitely aren't someone mom or dad would recognize."

Connor flinches. "Don't even go there."

"It's true," I yell.

He lurches to his feet, knocking his beer over in the process. His face is a thundercloud, his green eyes full of anger and pain. A tiny part of me feels badly for hurting him. The rest of me is too damn mad to feel guilty about it. He needs to hear the truth. He's strayed so far off the path, he's fifty miles into the forest at this point.

"What happens when it catches up with you, Connor?" I ask, trying not to yell this time. "What happens when you guys go too far and kill someone? Because that's where this road leads. The further you drift, the closer you get to the day you take someone's life. Is that really what you want?"

"I'm not a fucking murderer," he says.

"And a few months ago, you didn't attack innocent women either," I say quietly. "A few months before that, you didn't traffic drugs. Two years ago, your pawnshop wasn't filled with stolen property. Five years ago, you didn't do *any* of this."

"You don't know what you're talkin' about," he says.

"Yes, I do!" I cry. "They're turning you into someone else. You're a freaking criminal, Connor. You steal and sell drugs and beat people up. Now, you beat up innocent women too." I shake my head, tears of frustration burning at my eyes. "It has to stop."

"I've got shit to do," he mutters, grabbing his hat off the table. "I'm out of here."

I sigh in frustration, but don't try to stop him when he heads for the door. He's not going to listen to me. I think Andreas was right. Connor is in serious trouble. And I don't think I can save him this time. I don't think he *wants* to be saved.

"What am I going to do?" I whisper, sinking down into my chair once the front door slams behind him. Tears spill down my cheeks, grief welling up hard and fast. He's my only family, and I feel like I'm losing him.

You need to leave, little one. If you don't, he's going to drag you down with him.

I reach in my pocket and pull out the business card Andreas gave me last week. It's wrinkled beyond repair. I've kept it in my pocket all week, afraid if I left it out, someone would find it and know that he was here. I told myself to throw it away a thousand times, but I couldn't.

Every time I'd think about throwing it away, I'd think about his lips on mine or the way his arms felt around me, and I'd just...slip it back into my pocket. I'm not even sure why.

We're from two entirely different worlds.

We have nothing in common.

He's my brother's enemy.

But I don't think any of that matters because, right now, I desperately want to see him again. And not because I need his help either. I just...really want to see him.

Please don't let me regret this, I pray.

CHAPTER THREE
Andreas

I shouldn't have kissed her.

I should have put her on the back of my bike and gotten her the hell out of there.

Fuck. Why didn't I demand her number?

I pace around the living room, those three thoughts playing on an endless loop in my mind just like they have every other damn day for the last week. I'm slowly losing my fucking mind over Catriona Grady. Actually, scratch that. There's nothing slow about my descent into madness. I'm not sinking one level at a time like Dante travers-ing hell. I stepped off the ledge the second I set eyes on her and have been in a freefall ever since.

She's a beautiful little blonde with the greenest eyes I've ever seen. She had my dick hard as soon as I heard her voice. And then I got my hands on her. Every inch of her is soft and curvy, just right for a man like me to sink into. Feeling her up against me had me ready to come unglued.

And then I looked into her eyes. She was made for night, but she isn't moonlight, ephemeral and constantly chang-ing. She's the sun, vast and unyielding. The kind of light that burns bright and hot, eclipsing everything else. My entire universe reordered itself in that moment, stationing her right at the center of it.

I can't even explain it. I'm thirty-one years old, and I've never felt anything like that before. Ever. Realizing she isn't mine and I have no claim on her...my heart actually fucking *hurts*. Knowing she's tangled up with the Hell's Vipers has every protective instinct I have screaming in fury. I want her here with me, where I know she's safe.

But short of kidnapping her, there's not a whole lot I can do besides wait her out. Like with Autumn, she's skittish, nervous. God only knows what lies her brother and the Vipers have filled her head with about me and my brothers. If I push too hard, all I'm going to do is make her bolt. Or tip my hand to her brother and drag my brothers into a conflict we're trying like hell to avoid.

If patience is a virtue, I better be a motherfucking saint soon.

Staying out of Copper Creek is taking every ounce of restraint I possess. I know Catriona will come to me though. I've never been more certain of anything. She looked at me like she felt the same thing I did—the stirring of something deep and powerful, a desire to be closer to me that she couldn't explain. It spooked her, but she felt it.

I just have to wait for her to get curious enough to want to feel it again.

She's stubborn, but I didn't expect it to take quite this long. I may have to shackle myself in the basement if she resists much longer. Otherwise, I'll be showing up in Copper Creek again.

Cash is already pissed at me and Giant both for poking around over there in the first place. Not that I blame him. We let a teenager get the drop on us. Had she been one of the Vipers, our night would have ended a hell of a lot differently than it did.

One of these days, I'm going to stop letting my best friend talk me into doing stupid shit with him. Preferably before it gets us both killed.

"Fuck," I groan, grabbing the remote and clicking on the television.

"Please tell me you aren't about to watch Skinemax," Autumn says from behind me.

I turn to see her grinning at me from the bottom of the stairs, her hair in a messy bun on top of her head. Her pajamas have little ducks all over them. She always did love the damn things. I think they're part of the reason she fell in love with saving the world. She used to cry at the Dawn commercials.

"Skinemax?" I arch a brow, not entirely sure I even want to know.

"You've been cranky all week," she says with a shrug. "Porn is basically a happy pill. You should take like six of them and wake up less crabby tomorrow."

I stare at her for a long, silent moment. "There's so much wrong with that," I finally mutter. "But we aren't fucking talking about porn or sex or any of that bullshit. They don't even exist to you." I narrow my eyes on her. "They better not exist to you."

"I'm not talking about my sex life to you," she says, wrinkling her nose at me like she's not the one who brought up this conversation.

"You better not have a sex life, Autumn," I growl, my blood pressure rising. Jesus Christ. I know my sister is an adult, but she's still my baby sister. I don't want to think about some bastard taking advantage of her, let alone hear about it.

"Do you have a sex life?" she demands, her hands on her hips.

"Fuck no."

"Because it's rude to try to tell me what to do with... Wait. Seriously?" She blinks at me, clearly shocked. "You don't?"

I tip my head back and blow out a sharp breath at the ceiling. "Jesus Christ," I mutter, and then laugh. How did I manage to forget that Autumn has no boundaries and will ask whatever question pops into her head? She's always been that way. "New rule. We're not talking about my sex life, your sex life, porn, or anything remotely related while you're staying here. Some shit, I don't ever need to fucking know."

"Fine by me," she says. "I wasn't trying to have a conversation about it anyway, geez. I just made an observation supported by scientific fact, and you got all weird and cranky. Again."

I tip my head forward to glare at her. "I'm not cranky."

"Whatever you say, big brother."

The doorbell rings before I can say anything.

"I got it," Autumn says, skipping toward the door.

"Autumn, wait," I growl, hoping like hell it's Catriona...worried as fuck that it's her brother or someone else from his MC. It's nearly midnight. Catriona is too fucking innocent to be out this late by herself, especially with men like her brother's friends running loose. They aren't just troublemakers or young men raising a little hell. They're hardcore criminals.

I've seen what they've been doing for my father. Extortion and bribery are just the tip of the iceberg. And that's not even taking into consideration their business ventures with the Savages, who are involved in human trafficking and God only knows what else.

Autumn ignores me, quickly undoing the deadbolts and throwing the front door wide open.

Relief loosens knots in my shoulders when I see Catriona standing on the stoop, her arms wrapped around her, a black hoodie swallowing her petite frame. Her eyes are red as if she's been crying. When they land on Autumn, they widen, her mouth popping open.

"Oh," she whispers. "Um, I..." Her gaze darts toward me and then back to Autumn, trying to figure out who Autumn is and why she's here. I know the moment she reaches a conclusion. Panic fills her gaze, a blush staining her cheeks. I see the anger and the hurt in her eyes too. She's gotten it all wrong.

"Little one," I murmur.

"I shouldn't have come," she blurts, spinning away from the door.

"Catriona, stop."

"Holy crap," Autumn whispers. "You have a girlfriend."

I slide around her, grabbing Catriona before she can take off down the stairs. She struggles in my arms, fighting to get loose. Her round ass brushes my cock, turning him to steel.

"Stop fighting me, little one," I whisper in her ear, pulling her up against me. "She's my sister."

"Y-your sister?" she asks.

"Yes." I breathe her in, letting her floral scent work its way through my system. It soothes all those raw places a week without her inflamed. No, I'm not falling slowly. I'm plummeting at the speed of fucking light, fully prepared to crash land into love with this girl. The sooner I can get her on the same page, the better. "Her name is Autumn. She just moved back to Silver Spoon Falls."

"Oh," Catriona whispers, sagging in my arms. And then she whimpers my name. "Andreas? You...you were right. He is in trouble. I don't know how to fix it this time."

"Shh, little one," I croon, scooping her up as she starts to cry. "It's going to be okay."

"Is she okay?" Autumn whispers, peeking her head into the living room where I carried Catriona half an hour ago.

She's on my lap, her face buried in my throat. She's not crying anymore, but she hasn't made a move to pull away either. I'm just holding her, waiting her out. I think she needs to be held right now more than she needs to talk. She's a little koala bear, starving for affection. God only knows how long it's been since she last had any of that.

I jerk my chin in a nod, letting Autumn know she's all right.

Autumn crosses to us and places a washcloth and a glass of water on the coffee table for her. "Just in case," she mouths, and then squeezes my arm before slipping out of the room. She glances back at us once, her expression indecipherable, and then heads upstairs.

"Your sister probably thinks I'm a crazy person," Catriona mumbles.

"My sister knows what it's like to be in your shoes," I say, tucking silky strands of hair behind her ears. "Our father was a selfish man. He viewed the world as his playground and people as his toys. He hurt a lot of people, our mother and Autumn the most."

"I met him a couple times."

"I'm sorry," I say, meaning it. I doubt it was a pleasant experience for her. God knows, it wasn't for most people who crossed paths with him.

"Was he always like that?"

"Usually," I say. "But my mom loved him once. I figure that means he was someone worth loving at some point even if I never met that man."

"Oh. What happened between them?" she whispers, her voice raw.

I lean forward, grabbing the glass of water. "Here," I murmur, "drink this."

She obediently turns her head, allowing me to hold the glass up to her lips. She takes a couple small drinks before waving me off. "Thank you."

I replace the glass on the table. "My mom's family used to be in the shipping business in Greece. My father started gobbling up smaller companies over there, but he promised to leave their company alone if she married him. She believed him," I say, running my hands down her back. "He kept his promise for a while after they wed, but it didn't last long. Once he was sure she was in love with him, he took it without a second thought. By then, she was pregnant with me. I guess he thought she'd be too blinded by love to care, but it didn't work out that way. It destroyed her relationship with her family, and their marriage."

"Oh, wow." Catriona shifts in my lap, cuddling closer. "What did she do?"

"Named me Andreas," I say, smiling. "Her family never forgave her, but she never forgot them and never let my father forget either. She made sure he remembered what he did every single time he spoke my name—her family name."

Catriona lifts her head, blinking red-rimmed eyes at me. "Her family name was Andreas?"

"Mmhmm."

"You're serious."

"Family never meant much to him, but it meant every-thing to her." Oddly, he never tried to call me anything else. I'm not sure if using the name she gave me was his way of owning what he did or if it was a reminder to him that she felt something for him once. With him, who knows? He thought he could bully her into loving him again or buy his way into her heart. He tried everything under the sun except the one thing that might have actually saved their marriage. An apology.

"My parents died when I was twelve," Catriona says qui-etly. "Connor raised me."

Jesus.

I brush my thumbs down her cheeks, tracing the trails her tears left. Her skin is soft and warm.

She swallows, her pink tongue darting out to wet her lips. She doesn't ask me to stop, nor does she try to crawl out of my lap. Unable to resist, I trace the same path her tongue just took across her bottom lip, groaning at how soft it is, at how wet it is. My dick stiffens. And then stiffens again when her tongue peeps out, touching the side of my thumb.

"Little one," I whisper.

"Sorry," she says. We both know she doesn't mean it though. She wants me, perhaps as badly as I want her. But I don't want her in my bed because she's mad at her brother.

When she gives herself to me, I want it to be because she knows this is where she belongs. I want it to be because she can't imagine a future without me in it. Until then, I can't lose my head. This is too important.

"What happened tonight, Catriona?" I ask, steering us carefully away from the danger zone.

She deflates like a sad little balloon. "I asked Connor about the woman. You were right," she says sadly. "He knew about it. He was more upset that someone told me than anything else."

I want to ask for details, but I don't. As much as I want to know exactly what he said and what he knew, I can't ask her to betray her brother. Putting her in that position when she's already hurting would be wrong. I didn't bring her here to manipulate her into betraying him.

If I do that, I'm no better than the Vipers or my father.

I am who I am because I hold myself to higher standards. I refuse to be weak and selfish and take what I want, regardless of who gets hurt along the way. Far too goddamn many men in this world are like that. I won't be one of them, not when I've seen just how much damage they can do. My father trapped my mother by holding me and Autumn over her head. He had the money, the power, everything. Had she left, he would have taken us simply to punish her.

I was in college when she died. Autumn wasn't. He took his grief out on her, trying to mold her into a more obedient replica of the woman he'd lost. My sister was a toy to him, an instrument he used to get his way. He fully intended to turn her into a polite society wife and sell her into marriage to whichever family could do the most for his company, regardless of what she wanted.

She went through hell because she didn't trust that I'd protect her. She thought I'd side with him. The day she told me that, I made a vow to myself that I would never let myself become him. I'd do everything I could to be something better, and to fix everything he broke. People would always come first to me, no matter what. I won't change that now, not for any reason. Not ever.

I won't be him.

"I'm sorry," I say. "I know that had to hurt."

"You aren't going to ask if he was there?" Catriona eyes me doubtfully.

"No," I say gently, shaking my head. "I told you already. I'm different, little one. You'll tell me what you want to tell me and nothing more. You don't owe me answers or explanations. I didn't ask you to come here for that."

"Why did you ask me to come?"

"Your brother is in trouble," I say, choosing my words carefully. "Sooner or later, it's going to catch up with him. When it does, if you're there, there's nothing stopping it from catching up to you too."

"I haven't done anything wrong," she protests.

"You work in a pawnshop full of stolen goods. You spend a lot of time around the Vipers. Whether you're a member or not, I think you know how that looks for you." The police don't have to prove she stole anything or was otherwise involved in anything. Simply knowing they sell stolen goods where she works is enough to make her complicit. The fact that she's taken steps to cover for her brother makes her guilty of obstruction. When the feds make their move, they won't hesitate to round her up with everyone else if she gets in the way.

Her best shot—her only shot—is to walk away. I can protect her. She just has to let me.

"He's my brother," she whispers.

"I know." I rub her back, not without sympathy. For him, I have none. For her, my heart aches. She shouldn't be in this position. She's too goddamn young, too innocent.

She's quiet for a long, silent moment and then she sighs. "What do you need from me?"

"You can't go back."

"I know," she whispers. "I...um, I packed up my stuff before I left. He doesn't know I'm gone. We had a fight and he stormed out. I left a note."

"Did you tell him where you were going?"

She shakes her head. "I just told him that I was going to stay with a friend, and that I didn't want him to look for me." Her bottom lip quivers. "I left my cellphone behind so he couldn't track it. Um, I guess I need to find a place to stay. And a job. I have some money saved up but not much."

"You'll stay here."

She blinks at me. "I can't do that."

"You can."

"I cannot."

I smile at the shocked outrage in her voice. She's fucking adorable.

"Stay tonight then and we'll talk about it later," I say, unwilling to fight about it now. She will be staying here though. There's not a chance in hell I'm going to let her out of my sight. I just spent a week going out of my mind. No fucking thank you on doing it again. "All I want to know right now is what *you* need from me. What can I do right now to make it better for you?"

She sinks her teeth into her bottom lip, chewing on it. I gently pry it from between her teeth before she does any damage to it, not wanting her to hurt herself.

"Tell me," I command quietly, reading the anxiety in her eyes.

"H-hold me?" she whispers, almost like she's afraid to ask. And then she grimaces. "I'm sorry. I shouldn't ask you to do that. It's just...it's been a long time since anyone held me, and I feel...safe with you. Is that weird? That's probably weird, isn't it? Maybe I should just stop talking now." She places a hand on my chest, stretching like she's going to crawl out of my lap.

"Catriona, look at me."

She reluctantly lifts her gaze to mine, the lights in her eyes muted and dim.

"You feel safe with me because you are safe with me," I murmur, cupping her cheek in my palm to keep her from breaking my gaze. "You will always be safe with me, little one. And holding you damn sure isn't a hardship on my part, so stop thinking it is. But before we do that, I just want to make sure you understand something."

"Okay," she whispers nervously.

"I'll hold you for as long as you want me to hold you and I'll love every fucking minute of it, but I'm not making love to you tonight," I say, my voice firm. "So if that's what you're after, you need to put that thought out of your head right now."

"I..." Her cheeks turn pink, and she splutters.

"Just so we're clear, that's not me rejecting you," I say when she finally gives up and snaps her mouth closed. "I've been hard all fucking week, thinking about you."

"Oh," she whispers. "Then why?"

I tip my head down to hers, brushing a kiss across her lips. "Because I won't be something you regret tomorrow, little one," I murmur against her mouth. "When I'm in you, it'll be because you know we're forever. Just like I know it."

"Andreas," she gasps.

I kiss her again, a tiny peck to seal my confession, and then climb to my feet with her in my arms. "It's okay, rabbit. We've got time."

CHAPTER FOUR

Catriona

ndreas lives in the closest thing to a castle I've ever seen. Every room is more beautiful than the last with gorgeous marble floors, exquisite chandeliers, and incredible artwork adorning the walls. The place is massive. And yet it still somehow manages to feel like a home too. Everything is warm and inviting, made to feel welcoming and comfortable instead of like a museum. I'm not quite sure how that's possible, but it is.

"Oh wow," I whisper as he carries me into his bedroom. It's bigger than Connor's entire house. Moonlight spills into the room from large French doors and a massive skylight, giving it an ethereal glow. Thick white rugs cover the floor. A massive fireplace dominates one wall. The four-poster bed takes up another, sitting so high up I think I need a ladder just to climb into it. A chaise and a sofa are arranged off to the side in a private alcove. Dark furniture completes the room. It's masculine and beautiful at the same time.

"Come on," Andreas murmurs, gently depositing me in the bed.

I sink into the thick mattress like I'm sinking into a cloud. I flop backward with a soft laugh, flinging my arms out wide. If this is what it's like to be a billionaire...wow. Sign me up. My bed feels like a lame cot compared to this.

"You look like you're in heaven, little one," Andreas says, a crooked grin lifting the right side of his mouth.

"Close enough," I mumble. "This bed is amazing."

His dark chuckle rolls over me, turning my insides to mush. My stomach flutters at the thought of sharing this bed with him. Of feeling his arms around me all night. Maybe I shouldn't have asked it of him, but I couldn't help it. He asked me what I needed and that was the only answer I had for him. I need him to hold me together. I'm scared and I'm nervous and I'm sad and I'm angry and I'm a million different things that don't make much sense right now.

But when he touches me, none of that matters. I feel stronger in his arms, braver. All week, I convinced myself that maybe I just imagined feeling that way. But I didn't. As soon as he touched me tonight, I felt safe again, exactly like I did last week.

I'm pretty sure that means something.

"Come here," he murmurs, wrapping his hands around my hips and gently tugging me closer to the edge of the bed. Once I'm where he wants me, he quickly pulls my shoes and socks off, his fingers brushing my instep.

I giggle, squirming beneath him.

"Are you ticklish, little one?" He smiles down at me.

"Maybe a little."

His smile grows as he examines my chipped polish.

"I forgot to paint them," I mumble, though it's not entirely true. It's more like I decided not to paint them once the weather cooled. Who has time to paint their toes just to hide them in socks for the next five months? No one, that's who. If he's going to be looking at them, I'll be making time.

"They're perfect," he says.

I don't have to ask to know he means it. He's a billionaire, but he finds my ridiculous, chipped polish and chubby feet perfect. How is he real? What does he want from me?

Forever. Duh, my little voice whispers.

Like usual, I don't think it's wrong. I think he really means it when he says that's what he wants from me. That should probably freak me out. I'm nineteen. The only plan I've ever had for my life involved getting out of Copper Creek. Beyond that, there was nothing. I never let myself think that far ahead because I didn't want to get my heart broken when it didn't work out. In Copper Creek, things rarely work out.

But with Andreas...I feel myself stretching toward hope, reaching for something I never let myself even dream about before now. Not just a way out, but a real future with a home and a family and a *life*. Am I allowed to want that? Is it wrong to want it for myself even if it means leaving Connor behind? I push that worrying thought behind, refusing to dwell on it.

Tonight, I'm going to be a little bit selfish.

Tomorrow, I can go back to worrying about my brother.

"Raise up, rabbit," Andreas says, tugging on my pants.

I obediently lift my hips, allowing him to strip them off me. His eyes rake up my legs, heating to obsidian pools as they go. Part of me feels like I should cover my panties, hide them from his gaze...but I don't. I lay still, defiant in the virginal white cotton.

"Jesus," he mutters, his voice thick as he stares at me *there*. I know he sees the wet spot on them. He licks his lips when he sees it, his chest rising and falling. The way he looks at me... God, I've never felt more like prey before or less like running.

My entire body catches on fire. It takes every ounce of willpower I have not to squirm on top of the bed. But somehow, I manage to lay still.

"You're going to break me, aren't you?" he rumbles, lifting his gaze to mine.

I'm pretty sure he's going to break me first, but I don't tell him that. I just shrug, which makes him smile at me and shake his head.

"Fuck, yeah, you are," he says with a soft laugh. And then he reaches for my hoodie, slowly sliding it up my body. His lips touch mine in a reassuring kiss before he pulls it off over my head, leaving me in nothing but my panties and bra.

I tremble beneath him.

"Can I take your bra off, Catriona?"

"Y..." I swallow, working moisture back into my mouth. "Yes."

He kisses me again. My lips. My cheeks. Both of my shoulders. His stubble scrapes my sensitive flesh, making my stomach clench and twist and ache. God, it aches in the best way possible. I squeeze my legs together, trying to relieve the pressure.

"You're beautiful, little one. So fucking beautiful."

I tremble again when he strips my bra off in one deft move.

"My God," he groans, his breath blowing hot across my nipple.

I moan, arching beneath him, silently pleading for him to kiss me there. I want—no, I *need*—his mouth on me. Right there. I'm aching for it. Dying for it. What is he doing to me?

"Andreas."

"I know." He shifts around above me, his chest grazing mine.

I cry out, his name a broken plea on my lips. I don't even know what I'm pleading for here. More. Less. Everything. I want this man with an intensity that's almost terrifying. I've never felt anything like it.

"Lift your arms," he croons.

I obey as if in a trance...only to be left blinking in disappointed confusion as he pulls a t-shirt down over my head. His scent engulfs me, and I know it's his shirt. He's naked from the waist up, acres of olive skin and brawny muscle sending my mind into a tailspin. A single tattoo adorns his bicep. An intricate butterfly designed to look like a skull. It's haunting and beautiful at the same time.

"You should sleep, rabbit," he murmurs, lifting me from the bed and then pulling the covers back before gently laying me down again, my head against his pillows. "You've had a hard day."

"I..." He's stopping? Just like that?

He runs a hand down the side of my face, his onyx gaze eating me alive. "My control is paper thin when it comes to you. You're too goddamn beautiful."

My heart flutters.

He tips his head forward, pressing his lips to my forehead. And then the bedside lamp clicks off. I lay in quasi-darkness, listening to him shuffle around as he strips out of the rest of his clothes. My heart pounds against my breastbone, my body overheated. I still ache everywhere. I want him. Desperately.

He slips into bed behind me, pulling me into his arms. I melt into the hard wall of his chest, my back to his front. God, he feels even better mostly naked than he did fully clothed. He's warm and hard, his legs tangling with mine. I drift toward sleep, too exhausted to function.

His lips brush my shoulder. "Sweet dreams, little one."

I turn to tell him goodnight and something nudges my bottom, hard and insistent. He groans, grasping my hip to keep me still. Just like that, I'm wide awake again. He's hard. So hard. Doesn't it hurt?

"Catriona, little one," he says, his voice strangled when I shift my hips backward, trying to feel more of him. Curious, eager. I've never felt one before now. "Go to sleep."

"Sorry," I whisper. I'm not really sorry though. Not very anyway. He's the one who made me all achy and crazy and then just...stopped. As if I can just turn it off now that he's turned it on! I can't. My body doesn't work like that.

Until him, I wasn't sure it worked at all. I've been turned on before, sure, but never like this.

I scoot away from him several inches, putting a little distance between us.

He tries to pull me back into him, but I immediately scoot away again.

He sighs quietly but doesn't try to pull me back this time.

We lay in silence for a long time. I try to sleep, but I can't. I *feel* him in the bed with me. Eventually, I can't stand it anymore. It's too much. I slowly slip my hand between my legs, desperate to relieve a little of the pressure.

I'm so wet I should probably be concerned.

A tiny whimper escapes my lips when I slip my hand into my panties.

"Catriona?"

"Y-yes?" I whisper, my finger rolling over my clit. And oh God, I should stop. I know I should. But I do it again, too far gone to care if he's awake. If he knows what I'm doing.

"Are you fucking touching yourself?" he snarls.

I whine his name instead of answering, guilt crashing like cymbals in my chest.

"Jesus Christ," he says.

What am I doing?

Tears prick at my eyes.

"I'm sorry," I whisper, moving to pull my hand out of my panties.

Andreas grips my wrist in his hand suddenly, halting me. His breath comes in a ragged pant. "Finish it," he growls.

I freeze, barely even breathing. My gaze flies to his even though it's too dark to make out much of him. "W-what?"

"Finish it, little one," he demands. "Touch your little cunt until you cream all over your fingers for me. Let me hear how wet you are and how sweet you sound when you're crying out for me."

"Andreas."

"Do it, Catriona," he growls.

I jump to obey this time, circling my clit with my fingers. My back arches up from the bed, a whine leaving my lips. His hand is still locked around my wrist, almost as if he's helping me. It feels...dirty. Sexy. I moan his name, circling my clit again.

"Fuck," he grits out.

The bed shifts.

I cry out as he yanks my panties midway down my thighs, straddling my legs at the same time.

The lamp on the bedside table clicks on.

The first thing I see is the inferno blazing in his eyes. They're the blackest midnight, sucking me into forever. His cheeks are flushed, his face a thundercloud. He's not mad though, not really. He's so turned on he can't think straight.

My stomach clenches, arousal flowing between my thighs.

And then I see his fist wrapped tightly around his massive erection and swallow hard. He's...wow. I've seen porn before, but I always thought dicks were kind of ugly. Not his. It's beautiful, just like the rest of him. He's long and thick, the broad head slick with moisture. Thick veins run down the underside of his shaft.

"Play with yourself," he orders me, his eyes locked on my face. "Let me see you take yourself there while you're moaning my name."

Oh, God.

I sink my teeth into my bottom lip, my heart racing. He's watching me like he can't look away. It should make me shy and embarrassed, but it doesn't. Some unfamiliar part of myself bubbles to the surface, eager to please this man. That part likes the way he's looking at me as if I'm the only thing that exists in his world in this moment. That part wants to be a little bit naughty and touch myself while he watches.

I give myself over to that side, letting it guide me. I touch myself for him, shamelessly chasing every little ripple of pleasure, every gasp of delight. It's more intense with his eyes on me, way more than when I've touched myself alone.

"God yeah," he groans, working his hand up and down his shaft. "Look at you, little one."

I can't look at me. I'm too busy looking at him. He's beautiful as he pleasures himself. His face is a mask of agony, his gaze swimming with bliss. He works his cock hard, tugging and pulling roughly. I think he likes it that way. Rough.

Do I? I don't know.

Watching him, I think I might. The thought of him inside me, pumping his hips like he is right now, snarling and cursing, groaning my name. His hand in my hair, his lips on mine. Yeah, I like that. I like it a lot.

"Andreas," I gasp, so dizzy with pleasure it's a little bit frightening.

"Don't you dare stop, Catriona," he growls. "You don't stop until you finish what you started."

"I...I..." I try to tell him that it's too much, but the words get lost as a wave of pleasure buffets my body, my orgasm creeping closer, closer. So close I feel like I'm dancing on a razor-wire, spinning madly in circles as I try to keep from plummeting off the sides.

"Finish it," he commands.

I wail his name and let go, falling backward into bliss. Waves crash over me, dragging me down into a riptide of consuming pleasure. It's the most intense orgasm I've ever had. Somehow, I manage to keep my eyes on him, watching in a daze as he growls my name and throws his head back. His cock jerks in his hand, and then thick ropes of sticky cum land against my stomach and mound.

"Andreas," I moan, turned on all over again at the sight of him covering me in him.

He tips his head forward to watch too, his bedroom eyes at half-mast.

"Fuck," he groans, releasing his cock when the last drop lands against my skin. He stares at the mess he made for a long moment, breathing hard, and then he reaches out and rubs his cum into my skin. His eyes meet mine, swirling with hot possession. "I'm not washing it off. You're going to sleep covered in me tonight, little one."

"Good," I whisper. "Maybe then you won't regret it in the morning."

He falls forward, catching himself on his elbows at the last minute. "Regret it?" he says, capturing my lips with his in a hot, hungry kiss. "Little one, you'll be lucky if I let you leave the bed without a repeat performance in the morning."

"Really?" I ask, worried he's going to be mad at me. "You said you didn't want to have sex tonight."

"No, I said I'm not making love to you until you know this is forever," he disagrees, rolling us to the side and pulling me into his arms. "I'm not taking your cherry until you're ready for what that means. But play with that juicy cunt for me as often as you want. Just remember one thing."

"What?" I ask, my cheeks blazing with heat.

"If you touch what belongs to me, I set the ground rules. And my first rule is that you don't touch my pussy unless I get to watch you do it."

Oh. Oh, wow.

"Okay," I say, another frisson of heat waving through me.

"Goodnight, rabbit."

"Goodnight, Andreas," I whisper, burrowing into him.

Chapter Five
Andreas

"Rabbit, this is Jude Despora," I say, keeping Catriona tucked into my side when Fifth arrives at my office. "We call him Fifth."

"Hi," Catriona whispers, cowering into me like she isn't sure what to make of him.

Jude is...Jude. With wild hair, a scruffy jaw, and runway-worthy fashion sense, if anyone in the club should be teased about being a fucking model, it's him. But he's a big, grumpy son of a bitch. He tells it like it is and doesn't pull punches. His moral compass never deviates. He's the last motherfucker you'd expect to find in a courtroom...and the only motherfucker I'd want in one with me.

Which is exactly why I called him. I'm not going to keep Catriona a secret from the club or anyone else. I don't want anyone thinking I'm ashamed of her or trying to hide her. But I do want to know what exactly we're facing in terms of the case against the Vipers. Is she on the list of suspects? Are the feds going to come knocking? If anyone can sus out the particulars, it's Fifth.

"Hey, sweetheart," Fifth says, giving her a soft, encouraging smile. His gaze flits to me, rife with curiosity. I can tell he knows who she is, but he's a polite bastard around women. He won't make her feel anything less than welcome, regardless of how he really feels about seeing her cuddled up to me in my office. And I'm fully expecting him to be pissed about it. Me falling for the sister of a rival MC currently embroiled in a RICO case promises nothing but trouble for us.

"Jude, this is my girlfriend, Catriona Grady," I say, holding his gaze.

Catriona makes a soft sound that's partly a squeak and partly a stutter. It's fucking adorable. My girl isn't shy, but she's nervous as hell. I stayed home with her yesterday. But I nearly had to pick her up and carry her out of the house this morning to get her into my truck. She was adamant about staying at home by herself today. I think she's worried her brother is going to come roaring into town looking for her. But he has no reason to look here, not yet.

"Girlfriend, huh?" Fifth asks. "Does her brother know?"

"Not yet."

Fifth rubs his jaw, giving me an assessing look. "Plan on telling him?"

"Eventually," I say.

"What? Since when?" Catriona spins to face me. "We didn't discuss this."

"Are you mine, little one?" I ask, tipping my head down to look at her.

"I... Well, I..."

"You say anything but yes, and we're going to be kicking Fifth out of here while I prove it to you," I growl, narrowing my eyes on her. I don't give a fuck if we're in my office or not. I'll have her playing with herself and screaming my name on top of my desk until she's too blissed out to argue about it. "You're mine, Catriona. I don't give a fuck who your brother is or what he has to say about it."

"You can't just say things like that," she hisses at me, flapping her hands and shooting a horrified look at Fifth. "We have company, Andreas."

"It's my office. I can kick him out if I want."

"You're an overgrown bully, Andreas Romano." She peers at Fifth, anxiety in her gaze. "I'm sorry about him. He's just being grumpy, but he's not allowed to kick you out. I won't let him." She cuts her gaze at me, daring me to gainsay her.

"It's all right, sweetheart," Fifth drawls, amusement in his voice. "We stopped trying to teach him manners a long time ago."

"Her name is Catriona. Use it," I growl, not liking this *sweetheart* shit. I don't want anyone calling her anything but her name except me. Maybe that makes me an asshole. I don't care. She's got me all twisted in knots and turned inside out and upside down. I knew it the day we met. Spending the last two nights with her in my bed only made it worse.

She makes me...vulnerable in a way I'm not sure I know how to explain. I've never been in love before. I've never needed anyone like this or wanted to be everything for someone as badly as I want to be everything for this beautiful little light. She touches places that no one else does, rouses every instinct I have. I'm not just possessive of her, I'm ungodly protective of her too.

She's scared and anxious and out of her depth. And she's trusting me to keep her safe. I don't know what the Vipers put her through. But I know she doesn't trust easy as a result. I know she's leery of my brothers because of them. I trust my brothers implicitly, but she doesn't. Not yet.

Until she does, she needs me to set boundaries to see to her comfort. And I need to set them too. I need her to know that she can trust me to put her first in all ways just as badly as she needs to know she can trust me. Love is new to both of us. I'm not going to fuck it up.

"Jesus Christ." Fifth laughs loudly, shaking his head. "Another one bites the dust."

I shrug instead of denying it. I didn't bite the dust though. I ate a fucking crater in the ground.

"If I'm yours, does that make you mine?" Catriona asks suddenly, curiosity sparking in her green eyes.

"Are you admitting that you're mine?" I ask, smiling at her.

"Maybe," she mumbles, blushing.

I pull her to me, brushing a kiss across her forehead. "I already told you that I'm working on forever, little one," I remind her quietly. "I follow where you lead."

She melts into me for a moment, letting me hold her.

Fifth catches my gaze over top of her head, shaking his. He's not mad though. Concerned, maybe. I get why but the thing is...I don't fucking care. She isn't her brother, and his crimes aren't hers. If anyone understands how it feels to be judged guilty by association, I do. I've been there and done that. People still walk softly, expecting me to turn out like my father. It doesn't matter what I do to right his wrongs, I still carry that stigma.

I'm not going to let Catriona carry it too. She's innocent.

"Come on," I murmur a moment later.

I lead her to the conference table set up on the far side of the office, pulling her down into a chair beside me. Fifth takes a seat on the opposite side, facing us. I slide a legal pad across the table toward him in case he wants to take notes, though I doubt he'll need it. Fifth has the memory of a fucking elephant. He forgets nothing.

"Catriona worked at her brother's pawnshop," I say, getting right to it. "Strictly janitorial."

"Were you patched in, Catriona?" Fifth asks her.

"No, I wasn't a member of the MC," she says softly. "Connor didn't want me involved in what they did. Um, they were around a lot, but I never went to their clubhouse or anything like that." She chews on her bottom lip, looking between the two of us. "How bad is it?"

Fifth looks at me.

"Bad, little one," I murmur, turning her chair to face me. "I can't give you a lot of details, but they're involved with another club that's into some seriously heavy stuff."

"H-how heavy?"

"You don't want to know," Fifth says.

She looks to me for confirmation.

"The other club is involved in human trafficking," I say, unwilling to lie to her. "One of their members held a pregnant woman hostage after she got caught helping trafficking victims escape. Her baby was born with a congenital heart defect and nearly died. They killed her when she escaped to get the baby help."

Catriona pales slightly. "Did the baby–?"

"The baby is okay," I assure her. "Her aunt, Samara, has custody of her now. Samara just married Hands, our VP. You'll meet them sooner or later."

"Did Connor know about this?" she asks quietly.

"I don't know," I admit quietly. "As far as we know, the Hell's Vipers weren't involved with the trafficking scheme. But that doesn't mean they weren't aware of what the other club was doing. They've been running drugs for them. Possibly weapons too."

Catriona's eyes flutter closed on a sad sigh. "Connor, um, he's been selling drugs, I think."

Fifth glances at me.

"I overheard him talking to Rooster about moving product into Houston," she mumbles. "He never confirmed it when I confronted him about it, but I kind of figured that's what they were talking about." Her eyes pop open, focusing on me. "Why are you telling me this, Andreas? What are you asking me to do?"

"Nothing, rabbit," I promise. "We're not asking you to do anything. You don't owe me answers or explanations. You don't have to tell me anything about them or their business. I'm not interested in starting a war with them. Like I told you, the only thing I care about is protecting my people." I tip her chin up with a finger beneath her chin. "In case it's not clear, that includes you, rabbit."

Fifth clears his throat, claiming our attention. "Not to be an asshole here, but it'd help to know what she knows," he says with a shrug. "Might solve a few problems."

"No."

"I'm just saying, she has information we may need."

"You're rich," Catriona says to Fifth, eyeing him shrewdly. "Did you grow up that way?"

He tilts his head, a question in his eyes.

"Answer the question, please," she demands.

"I did," he says.

"Well, I didn't grow up that way. Silver Spoon Falls may be this wonderful town where great things happen, and rich people come to play, but Copper Creek has been dying since I was born," she says. "It's overrun by people willing to do whatever they have to do to get by, and by those eager to take advantage of that desperation to make a quick buck. Snitches are lucky if they get stitches in Copper Creek. Most of the time, they end up in ditches."

I reach for her hand, slipping mine into it.

"It's easy to do the right thing when you have the privilege and the power to do it safely," she finishes quietly, clinging to my hand. "Not all of us are that fortunate. Some of us grew up watching what happens when you speak up without either, and we just want to make it through the day alive."

Fifth is quiet for a minute, processing. And then he nods. "You're right," he says. "I did grow up in a different world than you, and I don't know what it's like to experience those struggles. It's not fair of me to ask you to put yourself at risk just to help make my life easier." He sighs. "But I'm not just asking for me, Catriona."

"Then why are you asking?" she demands.

Fifth looks at me, cocking a brow as if to ask if I'm going to tell her.

"Little one, you worked at your brother's pawnshop," I remind her gently. "You lived among the Vipers for years. When the police come knocking, it's quite possible they'll come with a warrant for your arrest too."

"But I already told you I didn't do anything," she protests.

"I know that," I say. "And the fact that you walked away helps. But if they decide they want to know what you know, they're going to back you into a corner and try to exchange your freedom for knowledge. They'll try to get you to testify against your brother and the Vipers by any means necessary."

"I..." She gapes at me. "Andreas," she whispers, her voice stricken. Tears well in her eyes. "Even if I told them everything I know, it wouldn't be enough to satisfy them. Connor kept me in the dark about all of it. I picked up bits and pieces here and there, but not about anything major. You know more about them than I do!"

"Hey," I murmur, pulling her out of her chair and into my lap. "Hey, it's all right." I wrap my arms around her, holding her tightly to my chest. "We don't even know yet if you're on their radar. That's why Fifth is here now. We're trying to come up with a game plan so we can do everything in our power to keep you out of it, okay?"

"I don't want to go to jail," she mumbles.

"Good, because I'm not going to let you go to jail."

I might, though, because I'm ready to break Fifth's fucking jaw.

"You ready to talk about it?" Fifth asks when Catriona slips into the bathroom fifteen minutes later. He knows exactly what's coming. I think he knew before he even pulled that bullshit.

"You're an asshole," I snap, glaring at him across the table. He intentionally backed her into a corner to see how she'd react to save herself. To see if she'd give up her brother if it meant keeping herself out of jail.

"I know," he says quietly, not denying it. "She doesn't know anything."

"I could have fucking told you that," I growl. "She isn't a criminal. She isn't a Viper."

"I won't apologize for caring about you, brother." He holds my gaze, his unyielding. "Two months ago, they attacked Kyra trying to get at Cash. They're shady, unscrupulous motherfuckers. They've got that girl tangled up in shit she has no business being tangled in. And she's their VP's baby sister. I wouldn't put it past them for a minute to send her after you to bring you down. I may be a bastard for making her cry, but I'd rather push now and know she's innocent than trust blindly and lose a brother," he says.

"She's scared out of her mind. You didn't fucking help."

Guilt crosses his face. "I know," he admits, blowing out a breath. "And I won't blame her if she hates me for pushing her. But you've been through the wringer already. We're not losing you to the fucking Vipers now."

"You aren't," I mutter. "She isn't one of them."

"I know."

"She's young," he observes.

I clench my jaw, refusing to acknowledge his point. She is young, goddammit. Far too young to be tangled up in this. Far too young to be mine. But I'm claiming her anyway. If that makes me an asshole, so be it.

I've worked my ass off to prove that I'm not my father. I've done more good in the year I've been in charge than he did in his lifetime. I'll keep doing good because it's the right thing to do. But if loving her is the thing that makes me irredeemable in the eyes of society, then fuck it. Love—real love, not the bullshit my father called love—isn't wrong. I refuse to believe it is.

"You're protective of her."

"Do you have a point?" I growl.

"Just an observation. Out of all of our brothers, there isn't one better suited to a girl like her," Fifth says quietly. "And there isn't another girl more suited to you. She's had it rough, but so have you. She's exactly who you need, brother."

"I plan on marrying her," I warn him.

He grins, shaking his head. "Figured as much."

"I'm not signing a fucking prenup either so don't even ask."

"What the fuck do all of you have against prenups?" he demands. "Goddamn. Cash and Hands both acted like I asked for their left fucking nut when I suggested it."

"You'll see," I mutter. When he falls—and fuck, I hope he falls flat on his face—he won't be interested in a damn prenup either. He's just like the rest of us, once he's in, he's all in. He's just too goddamn stubborn to admit it.

"The hell I will," he growls right on cue. "I'm not fucking getting married."

"Yeah, that's probably true." I smirk at him. "You'd have to find a woman willing to put up with your grumpy ass first. And we both know that's never going to happen."

He flips me off across the table, laughing. "I hate you."

"What happens now?" I ask, steering the conversation back to Catriona.

"Frankly, I don't think you have anything to worry about, Playboy," he says. "She's nineteen, and she's not a member of the MC. She was a janitor for the pawnshop. They'll have a lot more success trying to flip someone in the MC than trying to cut a deal with her. But I'll get in touch with my contact in Dallas and see what they have to say about her."

"Thanks, brother. I'd appreciate that."

"As far as her brother," he says and then sighs. "You need to prepare her for the fact that he's going down. Potentially for a long time. He's their VP. There's not going to be any talking him out of it. When they go down, he's going with them."

"Fuck," I curse. "I know."

Chapter Six
Catriona

"Would you stop introducing me to everyone as your girlfriend?" I whisper-shout at Andreas, who is seriously stressing me out. First, he introduced me to Jude as his girlfriend this morning. Now, he's formally introducing me to his sister as his girlfriend. Except there's nothing formal about it. She just walked in the front door two seconds ago.

"Uh, fuck no," he says, looking at me like I'm crazy. "Not unless you'd prefer future wife."

I whimper, burying my face in my hands. I think he's doing it on purpose. It's payback for touching myself the night before last...and again this morning. Though this morning was his fault. He woke me up kissing all over my neck and then slipped my hand between my legs and told me to make myself come.

Autumn laughs quietly, dropping her purse and keys on the table by the door. I'm not sure where she was yesterday, but she didn't come home until late last night. I think she was avoiding it to give us space. It made me feel bad. This is her home too.

"I'm not your girlfriend, Andreas," I say.

His growl is frightening. And sexy.

"We haven't even been on a date!" I cry, flinging my hands up in the air. "And you didn't even ask me to be your girlfriend. You just started telling people I'm your girlfriend. I'm pretty sure it doesn't work that way." I look to Autumn for confirmation. Hopefully she knows since I've never dated anyone before now.

"You've never taken her on a date?" Autumn spins to gape at her brother.

"Haven't had time," he mutters defensively.

"Unacceptable," Autumn declares, scowling at him. Dressed in a black business suit with red stilettos and matching lipstick, she's way more intimidating than I am. She looks like she's ready for a war in the boardroom. "You don't get to just tell her she's your girlfriend, Andreas Romano. This isn't kindergarten. You have to earn the right to claim a woman this beautiful. And you have *not* earned it." She huffs at him and then spins to me, looping her arm through mine. "Come on. We're going to get you ready while my idiot brother figures out where he's taking you tonight."

"But I..." Well, if it isn't the consequences of my own actions biting me in the butt. This isn't at all what I meant. I glance over my shoulder at Andreas, silently pleading for help as Autumn drags me up the stairs, but he just smirks at me. The big jerk.

"You'll have to excuse him," Autumn says, pulling me into her bedroom suite. Like Andreas's suite, hers is massive. It's not nearly as tidy as his though. She has boxes stacked in one corner, with clothes scattered around the floor. Her purple sheets are twisted up, one pillow hanging off the side of the bed. It's honestly a mess, but seeing it instantly puts me at ease.

At least something in his world is familiar. Everything else is shiny and perfect.

"He's a clueless idiot most of the time," Autumn says, releasing me to wade through the clothes in the floor on her way to the closet. "I don't think he's ever dated."

"Me either," I confess.

"Really? Why not? I mean, not that it's any of my business, but you're gorgeous."

"Thank you." I smile at her. She's genuinely nice. If she thinks it's odd that I showed up at midnight, had a meltdown, and then moved in, she hasn't mentioned it. "Um, my brother never let me date."

"My brother never let me date either." She scrunches up her nose in distaste. "Not that I ever wanted to date."

"Me either."

"Why not?"

"Men suck," I say with a shrug. The ones I know do anyway. Except for Andreas. He's...different. He doesn't make my skin crawl or make me want to vomit. His eyes aren't eternally bloodshot, and he doesn't constantly smell like alcohol and stale cigarettes. There's nothing juvenile or immature about him. And he doesn't have women hanging all over him all the time like the Vipers always do.

She laughs quietly. "I have a feeling I'm going to like you, Catriona Grady."

"I like you too," I whisper and then fidget nervously. "I've never really had any girl friends before. I mean, friends who were girls. Or friends at all, really." I bite my lip, figuring I probably shouldn't have admitted that. It probably makes me sound sad and desperate. It's true though. Sure, I had friends when I was a little girl. But they either moved away or stopped coming around once Connor got involved with the Vipers. For the past few years, I've been on my own.

"Then I'm thrilled to be your first girlfriend," she says with a bright, genuine smile. And then she gives a wicked laugh. "Now, *please* tell me that I get to help you get ready for this date because my brother has been a pain in the ass my entire life and I am dying to see him lose his mind over you."

"What do you have in mind?" I ask.

Her grin turns purely wicked. "Depends on how much you want to torture him."

I chew on my bottom lip, thinking it over. He did introduce me as his girlfriend twice today. And he made me go to work with him. Though I'm not really sure why since he didn't even do any work and we ended up leaving at noon.

After Jude left, I convinced Andreas to let me straighten up his desk. I don't know how he managed to find anything with it as messy as it was. I spent most of the morning organizing paperwork into chronological order. He spent most of the morning trying to interrupt me with kisses. I didn't complain too much. Kissing him is infinitely better than thinking about the trouble Connor is in.

For a long time, my brother was my hero. He's been slowly losing that status for a long time now. But I don't think I ever let myself grieve that loss until now. My brother isn't the man I always thought he was. He isn't a hero at all. He's a criminal, just like his criminal friends.

Part of me doesn't want to believe it. A big part of me rebels at the thought, refusing to accept that the same man who fought to keep me when anyone else would have given me up is the same one who now sells drugs and stolen property and hides his sins in the dark. But the rest of me...well, that part has been staring at the evidence for far too long to be so naïve. My brother joined an MC to find himself. Instead, I think he lost his dang mind.

I don't want to think about that tonight though. For once, I just want to be normal. I want to get dressed up and go out with Andreas and drive him a little bit crazy. I want to keep falling for the incredible man who burst into my life like a comet and turned it upside down. And I *am* falling. So fast it's a little bit terrifying and a little bit exhilarating at the same time. Andreas is everything I would have asked for if I'd known what to ask for in a man.

He says he wants forever...and I desperately want to give him that. But I'm so scared to let myself love him only to lose him. He wants me now, but what happens if I go to jail? Is it fair to take his heart if I'm only destined to break it? I don't know. Part of me thinks I should run now and protect us both. The rest of me thinks it's already too late for that.

Even if I go back home tomorrow, I'll still be leaving my heart here.

I'll still be taking his with me.

"Maybe just a little bit of torture," I whisper after a moment, earning a giant smile from Autumn. I send up a silent prayer that I don't end up destroying Andreas's heart and mine, but if God's listening, He doesn't answer.

"Stop staring at me," I whisper, squirming in the seat of the limo. My red bodycon minidress is beautiful. It's long sleeve, but plunges low between my breasts, showing more cleavage than I'm used to showing. The asymmetrical hem ends above midthigh, with a slit on one side that goes nearly up to my hip. It's sexy and daring, and Andreas can't keep his eyes off me.

He lounges across from me with his legs spread apart, one arm thrown over the back of the bench seat. He looks edible in his black tux. Then again, he usually does. The way he keeps looking at me is making me crazy. I'm not sure if he wants to spank me, kiss me...or fuck me. He growled when he saw me, and then spent five minutes trying to kiss my lipstick off.

He wasn't very happy with his sister when it wouldn't come off, which she thought was hilarious. I don't think he's very happy about how short my dress is either. He kept asking Autumn where the fuck the rest of it went. Eventually, she smacked him in the back of the head and then said something to him in Italian that I didn't understand.

He got real quiet after that and told me how beautiful I look.

I have no idea where he's taking me, but I know we're going to Houston. Hearing that made me feel better about the whole situation. I'm not ashamed to be seen with him. I'm just...worried. My brother already hates him. The last thing I want is for Connor and the Vipers to pick a fight with Andreas and the Silver Spoon MC because I left home. Things between them are bad enough without adding fuel to the fire.

Sooner or later, I'm going to have to tell my brother that I'm dating Andreas. But I don't want him to find out because we were seen together. Or, worse, because we ran into him while we were on my first ever date.

"I couldn't take my eyes off you if I tried, rabbit," Andreas rumbles, swallowing hard. "Had I known Autumn was going to turn you into a fucking Goddess, I would have rescued you instead of letting her have her way."

"Andreas," I say, laughing softly. "It's just a little makeup and a dress."

"No," he disagrees, shaking his head. "It's you, Catriona. You're so fucking pretty. Jesus. You're pretty enough to tempt a saint. And I've never been a holy man, little one."

I smile shyly, my nerves settling. "Then I guess it's a good thing I'm not expecting a saint tonight, isn't it?" I ask.

"No?" His lips quirk up into my favorite crooked grin. "What are you expecting, rabbit?"

"I don't know. I've never been on a date before." I glance at him from beneath my lashes, nibbling on my bottom lip. "But I'm kind of hoping that maybe..."

"Maybe what?"

"Maybe..."

His hands flex against the leather seat. Oh, he's so impatient and bossy! I *love* knowing that I can shake his composure the same way he rattles and shakes me. He's a freaking billionaire. He's so cool and confident and put together, and I'm just a curvy nineteen-year-old from a one-horse town. On the surface, we're polar opposites. There's nothing about us that fits...and yet *everything* about us fits.

Knowing he's as affected by me as I am by him bolsters my confidence. It makes me feel alive in a way I never have before. It makes me feel womanly in a way I never expected. With Andreas, I'm not just a curvy nineteen-year-old girl. I'm a powerful, desirable woman. One this man finds irresistible.

"Maybe," I say, sliding out of my seat and swaying toward him.

He reaches for me, pulling me down to straddle his lap. I twine my arms around his neck, groaning when he spreads his legs apart slightly to force my dress up higher on my thighs. I know he can see my panties. I think that was his entire plan.

"Maybe what, little one?" he rasps in my ear, his hands like vises around my hips. He's panting like he's out of breath, his eyes on fire. God, he's so damn sexy like this.

"Maybe I won't have to touch myself when it's over," I whisper.

"Fucking Christ," he growls, his grip tightening on me. He sits perfectly still.

For a minute, I think maybe I pushed too far and asked for too much. He's really not going to touch me at all until I agree to give him forever. Part of me wants to cry out in disappointment. The other part thrills that he wants forever so fiercely that he's willing to deny himself even a taste of pleasure to get it.

"You want me to touch you?" he asks then.

"Yes," I sob, relief and need crashing together, creating a harmonic that feeds off one another. "I need you, Andreas."

He groans my name, yanking me forward. I fall into his chest, landing with his lips against mine. He kisses me like he plans to steal my soul and claim it as his own. It's hot and heavy and dark. God, he's so good at kissing me breathless. I don't just submit to him. I give myself over to him entirely, letting him consume me.

"Oh!" I cry, sobbing into his mouth when he plunges one hand between us, deftly pulling my panties to the side. Part of the fabric tears. His thumb parts my bare slit. I'm already dripping wet for him, pleading for release. I've been that way since he kissed me once Autumn finished my makeover.

"Fuck," he groans. "Are you hurting for me?"

"S-s-so bad!"

"Show me," he demands. "Ride my hand."

I have no idea how to do that, but I'm willing to figure it out in the name of science. And orgasms, of courses. I shift on his lap, trying to plant my legs against the seat to give myself a little leverage. Between his height and my dress, it's virtually impossible.

"Use me, little one," he says. "Hold onto my shoulders and rock your hips. I won't let you fall."

I do as instructed, gripping onto his shoulders and rocking my hips.

"Good girl," he croons.

And oh. Is that supposed to make my stomach clench and quiver? I'm not sure, but I like the way he says it like *I'm* pleasing him even though he's the one touching me.

"Andreas," I gasp. Touching myself with him watching was intense, but this is an entirely new level of pleasure. His hand between my legs feels so much better than mine. He knows exactly where to touch me and how to touch me to send shards of pleasure dancing through my veins. If the limo driver can hear us through the privacy screen, he's hearing an awful lot right now.

"Do you have any idea how hard you make it to keep my dick out of you?" Andreas rasps, his voice like smoke. One thick finger teases at my entrance before gently slipping inside.

"No," I moan, riding his hand like my life depends on it.

"I'm hard every fucking minute of the day since I met you," he growls, rolling his thumb over my clit. I'm so wet, there's no hiding the sounds my body makes as I rock against his hand. "I want to plant my kid in you more than I want my next breath. I should be ashamed of myself for how badly I want to tie you to me." He presses his face against my chest, running his lips along the cleavage that spills from the top of my dress. He nips my skin between his teeth.

I cry out, lifting up and then falling back down. He curls his finger up, touching some spot inside that connects to every nerve ending in my body. They all light up at once, firing, firing, firing. I explode apart at the seams, shattering into a thousand tiny pieces. I spin and twist and roll through a fog of ecstasy, whimpering his name.

He holds me through it, sheltering me in his strong arms. "Good girl," he breathes against my ear, dropping kisses into my hair. "Ride it out, little one."

I do, every perfect second. And then I frown.

"Are you ashamed?" I whisper, nestled in his arms, my legs draped across his.

"Fuck no," he says, making me smile. "You're mine. Once you're ready for me, I won't be moving slow or taking prisoners. I'm not stopping until you're tied to me in every single way imaginable."

"Do I get a say in this?" I ask, fighting a smile.

"I'm not in you right this second because I'm giving you time to have your say," he growls, something deep and powerful glittering in his onyx eyes. "Once I take that cherry, we're permanent. I'll pluck the damn stars from the sky to make you happy. I'll walk through hell to keep you safe. Whatever you want, I'll give you. But the one thing I won't be doing is surviving without you, rabbit."

"Andreas," I gasp, blinking rapidly as tears fill my eyes. That's the craziest, most ridiculous, absolute sweetest thing I've ever heard. And I know he means it. It's written all over his face.

"You're not surviving without me either, Catriona," he says, brushing his thumbs beneath my eyes. "Every day without me, breathing will hurt a little bit more. You need me, little one. Just like I need you. You might not be ready to admit it yet, but you feel me. Right here." He places his palm over my pounding heart.

"H-how do you know?" I whisper.

"Because it's my home," he says, taking my hand in his. He spreads my fingers out and then presses my palm to his chest, my fingers splayed wide across his sternum. "And this is yours."

CHAPTER SEVEN

Andreas

"I don't think we're supposed to be here," Catriona whispers, glancing furtively around as I pull her past a barricade outside of the Toyota Center in Houston. Everyone else is bypassing the entrance, heading down the street in a steady stream. But everyone else isn't good friends with Declan "Bender" Valentine, lead singer of Bent, the band playing tonight. He's one of my brothers, a member of our MC.

He's got a security guard waiting at the door to let us in. I'm not sure how Catriona feels about rock music, but everyone loves Bender and his bandmates. I want our first date to be one she never forgets. Dinner with Bender, followed by front row seats to the show will be an experience to remember. She deserves that. She hasn't had many of those in her life.

Autumn would probably lose her mind if she knew this was what I came up with for the night. It's over the top. But fuck. I didn't bring Catriona here to impress her. I don't want to wine and dine her and dazzle her with sights that will only remind her of just how small her world has always been.

I want to share her with the people who matter, the ones who will help me love her the way she deserves. The ones who will help protect her and show her that she can fit into this world too. Bender is part of my world. When she marries me, he'll be part of her world too. She needs to meet Bender before she sees him on stage so she can meet the stubborn, selfless pain in the ass I know, not the rockstar the rest of the world knows.

Our MC is a brotherhood. We're a family. I want her to be comfortable with my brothers. I want her to know that she can count on them to have her back, no matter what. We aren't the Vipers, and she doesn't need protection from them. She doesn't need to fear them. She damn sure doesn't need to feel like she's less than them.

"Trust me, little one," I murmur, shooting her a confident grin.

She gives me a look that makes it clear she thinks I'm violating every rule in the book, but she lets me lead her around the barricade. I fight a smile the whole time. I fucking love that she's a stickler for the rules.

If I ever come face to face with her brother, I may break his fucking jaw on principle. He never should have gotten involved with the Vipers when he had her to think about. He certainly never should have had her working in his pawnshop or covering for him. God only knows how long she did it or how many times she lied his way out of trouble. She loves him fiercely, and he used it to drag her into something that's so far outside of her character it's a goddamn travesty.

Thank God, Giant talked me into taking a ride. Thank God, we decided to snoop around the pawnshop. Thank God, Catriona confronted us. Thank God, she came to me for help. Until last week, I always believed we were the masters of our own fate like Henley wrote in *Invictus*. Now, I'm not so sure. If fate didn't play a hand at throwing us together, I'm not sure what did.

"We're going to get in trouble," Catriona hisses, tugging on my arm as a cop car turns onto the block. "I can't go to jail with torn panties, Andreas."

As if I'd let her go to jail at all.

"Relax, rabbit," I murmur, rapping on the glass door. Unlike the other, more elaborate entrances to the stadium, this entrance consists only of two sets of double doors. "We're exactly where we're supposed to be."

"You still tore my panties," she mumbles, making me chuckle. If she's expecting an apology, she'll be waiting a while. I don't regret tearing her panties in the least. Keeping my hands off her is going to be a serious problem. She's a little temptress when she wants to come. I'm not nearly strong enough to tell her no. If she doesn't fall for me soon, we're going to be in serious fucking trouble.

"Keep being fucking cute and I'll tear every pair you own," I tell her, smirking.

"You will not!" she gasps.

"Try me, rabbit."

She narrows her eyes on me, her chin coming up. "Fine," she says. "Go ahead and tear them. And then you can explain to the whole world why they keep seeing my butt every time I wear a dress." She presses up against me, her gorgeous tits smashed onto my arm. "And just so you know, I plan to wear *lots* of dresses, Andreas Romano."

"New rule," I growl, plunging my hand into her hair and tipping her head back until my mouth hovers inches from hers. "If anyone sees what belongs to me, you'll spend the next three days wearing nothing but my handprints and my cum."

She moans softly and then something...contemplative flashes in her eyes. "Wait. Does that include tonight?"

Does that include...?

Jesus Christ. She's trying to kill me.

"Little one?"

"Hmm?"

"Kiss me before you make me stand my brother up," I say, chuckling.

"Fine," she mutters. "But you still owe me new panti–"

I cut her off with my lips on hers. By the time I let her up for air, the security guard is at the door, and she's forgotten that she's disgruntled over the hole in her panties.

"Hi," she squeaks to the security guard, blushing profusely. "Um, I'm pretty sure we aren't supposed to be here, but he doesn't listen to me." She jerks her thumb at me.

"'Sup, Playboy?" Grizz says, grinning at me.

"Good to see you," I murmur, sliding my palm against his then pounding our fists together. Like a lot of the guys who do security at shows here, Grizz works for Giant's company, Carmichael Security. They specialize in protection for people like Bender, celebrities with massive followings. Grizz is a fucking behemoth. No one gets past him.

"Of course you know him," Catriona says, sighing dramatically.

Grizz looks at her then back to me. "This one's yours?"

"Working on it."

"Nice," he says. "He's waiting for you guys. You need me to take you up?"

"Nah. I know where to find him," I say.

"Here." Grizz hands me two VIP passes. "Just in case anyone gives you a hard time."

I snort but take the passes anyway. When your face is plastered everywhere as often as mine is, people tend to know your name. And if they don't remember your name, they're smart enough to find someone who does before they stop you. I can't recall the last time someone questioned whether I was allowed to be somewhere. I could be on my way to rob the place, and most people would happily show me the way. It's goddamn ridiculous, honestly.

"Holy crap!" Catriona whisper-shouts.

I glance down at her.

"Bent is playing here tonight." She points at the giant banner stretched across the far wall. Bender's ugly mug is front center, his long hair, and dark eyes unmistakable. Women go fucking crazy over him. It's great for me. When he's around, everyone leaves me alone and bugs the hell out of him instead.

"Mmhmm," I say, chuckling. Most women would have asked a million questions by now about our plans for the night. Not Catriona. I think if I were anyone else, she'd have asked just as many questions and wouldn't have been satisfied until she had answers. But she knows she's safe with me. She trusts me to take care of her. "I thought you might like to meet Bender, little one."

"You know Bender?" She gapes at me.

"He's one of my brothers.

"Really? He's the one we're here to meet?"

"Yep."

"Catch y'all later," Grizz says.

"Thanks, man."

He gives us a two-finger salute and then takes off. I lace my fingers through Catriona's and head toward the stairs to go find Bender. The stadium is home to the Houston Rockets, so everything is decked out in team colors and memorabilia. Catriona barely notices. She walks quietly at my side for a moment and then peers up at me, her lip caught firmly between her teeth.

"You're a billionaire," she says. "Bender is a rockstar. Giant is...I'm not sure what he is, but he's something. Jude is a lawyer. Are there any normal people in your MC, Andreas?"

"Normal people?" I laugh quietly, leading her up the stairs to the second floor of the stadium.

"You know what I mean." She rolls her eyes at me.

"We're all normal, rabbit," I murmur. "We've just been fortunate in life."

"So that's a no then," she says, making me smile again. She's cute when she gets all snarky and sassy. "You're all ridiculously hot and crazy successful, aren't you?"

"First of all, I'm the only one you're allowed to look at," I say, hitting her with a hard look. "Everyone else in the MC looks like Peewee fucking Herman as far as you're concerned. Second, we're all successful, yes. But success looks different to each of us, rabbit. If Hands was asked to give up his practice to save even a single patient, he wouldn't hesitate. Hacker's family is probably worth more than mine. He could dominate the tech industry if he wanted to do it, but he's happiest here."

"I didn't mean it like that," she says softly.

"I know," I promise. "But my point is, each of us defines what success looks like to us and it's different for each of us. To me, success isn't money or power, little one. It's repairing the damage my father did to our company and our family. It's having a family of my own. It's love."

It's growing old with her. It's spending the rest of my life loving her.

Her expression softens, anxiety and consternation melting away.

"I don't want you worrying yourself, thinking you won't fit in because you aren't a millionaire or didn't come from money or don't own a company or haven't figured out exactly what your life is going to look like fifteen years from now," I murmur, gently tugging a loose curl as we reach the top of the stairs. "We're all still figuring shit out. We all want different things and we're all on our own paths to reach them. My brothers and I are just lucky enough to travel alongside one another along the way."

She stops walking and tips her head to the side, looking at me with wide eyes. "You're pretty smart, Andreas Romano."

"Yeah?" I grin at her.

"I mean, I'm pretty sure you're full of it, but you sure look pretty saying it," she says, and then squeals with laughter and dodges away from me when I try to get my hands on her. "I was just kidding!"

"You were not, you little liar."

"You're right. I wasn't. You did look pretty saying it," she says, laughing up at me with greenest eyes and the brightest smile I've ever seen.

I stop chasing after her. I stop moving altogether and just fucking...stare, completely transfixed by her. My heart rolls over, tumbling out of my chest directly into her delicate little hands. When it does, I realize something so blatantly obvious I don't know how I missed it at all.

The last week of my life has been the best week of my life, hands down.

"And I'm caught up in an avalanche but I'm still going nowhere fast, trying to get to you," Catriona belts out, her beautiful voice ringing through the Lexus Lounge.

"Holy shit," Bender says, staring in shock at her from across the table. "Your girl has pipes, brother."

Fuck yeah, she does. Jesus. Her voice is incredible.

"I didn't know she could sing like that," I murmur, watching her as she fumbles the lyrics and laughs it off with his drummer before launching into the chorus. Everyone at the table is watching her and smiling. She's so fucking happy, so beautiful. She lights up the entire room.

"Let me bring her on stage," Bender says.

I quickly shake my head, earning a scowl from him.

"Don't be a jealous asshole," he says, his voice soft so it doesn't carry. "With a voice like that, she could go far, man. Don't be the dick who holds her back because you don't want to share her."

I don't want to share her, this is true. But I'd rent out entire stadiums and pack them with people if she wanted to sing in front of crowds. I'll support her no matter what path she chooses in life. I don't think that is what she wants for her life though. More than anything, Catriona craves affection and stability and the freedom to make her choices.

"You know me better than that," I mutter and then quickly fill him in on the situation. Since he's been on tour, he's only gotten bits and pieces of what's been going on at home. Aside from sneaking home for Cash's wedding, this is his first time back in the state in a while. He probably won't make it back home until Thanksgiving next month. He's out of the loop. Especially on more recent developments.

"Damn," he breathes once I've given him the highlights. He shakes his head, glancing at Catriona. "Her brother sounds like a fucking asshole."

I grunt my agreement.

"What do you need?" Bender asks.

"This right here." I nod my head in her direction. Two days ago, her world crumbled around her. This morning, it crumbled again. But tonight, she's laughing. She's happy. She needed a night of normalcy, one where she didn't have to worry about her brother or the Vipers or think about what happens next. For tonight, she just needed five minutes to breathe. And I needed it for her.

"The rest of the MC met her yet?" Bender asks, his expression softening as he watches her. He can be an arrogant asshole. It comes with the territory when the whole world is screaming your name every night. But he's got his head on straight and never let fame change him. It never turned him cynical or hardened his heart.

"Not yet. I'm introducing everyone slowly to give her time to adjust."

"Good idea," he says, spearing a piece of steak with his fork. "It'll make it far easier for me to steal her from you if there's less competition from those assholes."

"Have you ever tried to sing opera?" I ask, eyeing his steak knife. "Because you keep talking that bullshit and you'll be singing it tonight, fucker."

He grins at me, his eyes glittering with amusement. "So it's like that, huh?"

"Yeah," I say quietly. "It's exactly like that."

He smacks me on the back and then laughs loudly. "Jesus Christ. I don't know what the fuck you guys are drinking, but you're dropping like flies. I'm scared to come home. My ass may end up married by the new year at this rate."

"Aww," Catriona says, her eyes lighting up. "You're getting married?"

Bender shoots her a look of horror, which makes his bandmates crack up. He's been more than vocal about his feelings on the subject. The last time a reporter asked if he'd ever get married, he laughed for so long she got pissed and stormed out of the interview. "Uh, fuck no. I'm never getting married."

"Oh." Catriona scrunches up her face in confusion. "Didn't you just say you're getting married by the new year?"

"Not me," he says, quickly shaking his head. He looks pointedly in my direction. "Maybe someone else though."

"Andreas," she groans, placing her palms on her cheeks. "Please tell me you didn't tell him that we're getting married!"

"What the fuck?" Bender blinks at me. "You're getting married?"

"No!" Catriona shouts.

"Yes," I growl, narrowing my eyes on her. She better not have a thing for Bender or I will spank her perfect little ass.

"No, we are not!"

"Yes, we are, little one."

"You...you..." She splutters, staring at me like she isn't sure if she wants to laugh or cry or just give up and change the subject. I fucking love rattling her. She gets so cute when she's flustered. "I'm telling your sister!"

"Oh, busted," Bender says, laughing his ass off.

I flip him the bird.

"We are not getting married," Catriona announces to the table at large, her eyes wide and her cheeks as red as that lipstick that won't come off and her dress. "He hasn't even bought me a ring or asked me, and I can't get married without a ring. It's a whole thing in the ceremony!"

Jesus.

My heart literally stops for a full beat before it lurches into action again. Is she saying...? Does she mean...? Fuck, she does, doesn't she?

Bender looks at me and then laughs loudly and reaches for his beer. "Yeah, there's definitely something in the fucking water back home," he says.

I push away from the table, hauling myself to my feet. Catriona is going to be disappointed but seeing Bender and the band play is just going to have to wait for another time. We've got something more important to do right now.

I stomp around the table to her, drawing to a stop behind her chair. "Little one."

"What?" she cries, flinging her hands up in exasperation, which makes Penelope laugh. Being the only woman in the band, she's surrounded by nothing but men and screaming fangirls while on the road. I think she's loving having Catriona here.

"Say bye to your new friends, rabbit. We're leaving."

"We're leaving?" Catriona cranes her neck to look up at me. "But I thought..." Whatever she sees on my face has her objection dying on her lips. She swallows hard, her pulse hammering in her throat. Her green eyes heat and darken as she stares at me. "Bye, new friends," she whispers, not even breaking eye contact with me.

I lift her out of her chair, fighting like hell not to lose it before I get her alone. I haven't even touched her and I'm already shaking. So is she. She knows this is forever. She wants to marry me. Fuck.

You're mine now, little one.

Chapter Eight

Catriona

"Where are we?" I ask Andreas, wandering around the luxury penthouse in uptown Houston. A wall of glass stretches the length of the living room, offering a breathtaking view of the city. Thick rugs cover wooden floors, with pretty glass tables carefully arranged around the room. A large sectional takes up most of the living room, looking both luxurious and inviting. I've never seen decadence like this.

"This is my place, little one," Andreas murmurs, coming up behind me. He turns me toward a window and points toward a body of water off in the distance. "That's the Buffalo Bayou. If you follow it east to the Houston Ship Channel, you'll find our biggest shipyard."

"Oh," I say. I guess I never thought about where else his company was located or where he stayed when he visited those locations for work. "How often do you stay here?"

"Not often. I prefer to work from the office in Silver Spoon Falls." He wraps his arms around my waist, pulling me up against him. I melt into his chest, staring at our reflection in the window. We should probably look mismatched and silly together, but we don't. I think we look kind of beautiful together. Even though I'm curvy, his sheer size dwarfs me, making me seem smaller, more delicate. In my borrowed dress, I look bold and daring, sexy. The deep red color matches his tie perfectly.

"Why are you so afraid to admit that you're in love with me?" he asks.

"I..."

"I know you are. I see it in your eyes when you look at me," he murmurs, pressing his lips to the side of my throat. "I feel it when you touch me. I hear it when you say my name. You love me." His tongue dances up the tendon in the side of my neck, causing my knees to wobble. "You want to marry me."

"Andreas," I say. It's the only thing I know to say. Because he's right. But I can't tell him that and I won't lie to him either. I do love him, so damn much. I do want to marry him; more than I think I've ever wanted anything. After my parents died, I used to pray every night for God to please bring them back. Every single night for two years, I prayed. In two days, I think the way I need Andreas supersedes even the most fervent of those prayers.

But he knows what it's like to lose people too. He knows what it's like to be alone and to be sad and to pay for the sins of others. He's been through so much in his life and he's fought so hard to overcome it. He could have anything in this world. Yet all he wants is to fix the things his father broke—to repair the reputation of his company, to regain the trust of his employees, to heal the hurt his sister feels.

He's selfless and beautiful and the best man I've ever known. How am I supposed to take his heart and his name if I'm only going to bruise one and tarnish the other? That's not fair to him. He's been better to me than anyone ever has. I don't want to repay him by destroying what he's worked so hard to build.

"Tell me why you're afraid to love me," he demands.

"I'm not afraid to love you," I whisper, watching his face in the mirror. He isn't going to let me wiggle out of this one. Not this time. "I'm afraid to let you love me."

He blinks those ridiculously long lashes and then gently turns me to face him. "Explain."

I sigh quietly. "You're already paying for sins that aren't yours, Andreas. If you're with me, even if I don't go to jail, once people find out about my brother, they're going to judge you. Especially if anyone finds out about your father's connection to the Vipers. You've worked so hard to repair the damage he did. I don't want to be the thing that destroys it."

"No."

"No?"

"No," he says again.

I blink at him. "What do you mean 'no'?"

"I mean no, little one," he says, tipping my face up to his with a finger beneath my chin. "Do you know how many perfect moments I've had in my life? Six, rabbit. I've had six." He brushes his lips across mine. "Every single one of them has been since I met you. So no, I'm not going to stand here and let you think for even a second that having you in my life could ever make it worse or destroy it or make it anything less than the absolute gift it is. *You* are a gift. The time I spend with you is a gift. Every memory I make with you is a gift. Nothing will ever change that."

"Andreas," I whisper, my heart fluttering as tears spring to my eyes. How does he do that? Every time I think he can't get more perfect, he somehow does. I've never been someone who cries at the drop of a hat. But lord, this man knows how to hit all of my buttons. "I'm scared."

"I know you are." His lips brush mine in another intoxicating pass. "But that's what you have me for, rabbit. Let me be your strength. Trust me to get us through this. It might not be okay today or tomorrow or even next week, but it will be okay. I won't rest until it is."

"I don't want to hurt you," I whimper, twisting my hands up in his jacket, pulling him closer, closer. He'll never be close enough. He'll never kiss me enough. I'm greedy when it comes to him. So damn greedy. I've tried so hard not to be selfish with him, to stand firm and guard his heart as fiercely as I can. But my resolve is weak. I'm weak when it comes to him. So damn weak.

"The only thing that hurts me is you thinking you don't deserve me." His nose glides along mine, his breath blowing hot across the side of my face. It sends pleasurable chills through me, hardening my nipples, heating my core. His hands skim my body, tugging at the fabric of my dress, gliding like silk across my bare skin. "You're the brightest light in this world, little one. I saw you shining in the mouth of that alley and thought you were a fucking angel. I knew then that you were mine. I love you, rabbit. Let me love you."

"Oh no," I whisper, tugging the button free on his jacket and then slipping my hands beneath. I run them up his chest and then over his shoulders, slipping his jacket down as I go. It slides over his back, hangs on his arms, and then slips free, landing on the floor at our feet.

"Oh no?" he murmurs, planting sweet kisses all along my jawline.

"I forgot you could see me where I was standing in the alley."

He huffs out a laugh. "I tell you I love you, and this is your response? You're killing my ego, rabbit."

"It seemed important," I mutter defensively. "I thought you and Giant were kidnappy murderers. Letting you see me probably wasn't smart."

"Jesus," he groans, burying his face in my throat. "I'm never letting you out of my sight again, Catriona. Had anything happened to you..."

I don't remind him that something did happen to me. He got the drop on me. I have a feeling that won't make him feel any better.

"I love you, Andreas," I whisper instead, not sure it's adequate to express the way I feel about him. There's so much, it feels like a tempest raging through me. A million different emotions pulse through me with each electric beat of my heart—hope, want, need, desire. So much damn desire.

I'm not entirely convinced that loving me won't hurt him, but I think I have to take a leap here because I'm already hurting him. Pushing him away is hurting him. Holding part of myself back is hurting him. What's the point of trying to save him from a possibility when doing so causes an inevitability? I don't want to cause him pain. I don't want to be the thing that makes him sad. I just want to be with him. I just want...forever.

If asking for that is wrong, well, I guess I'm just going to have to be wrong.

"Andreas?"

"Yeah, little one?"

"It's my turn to make a rule now."

"Yeah? What rule is that?"

"If I'm going to wear pretty dresses for you, you have to leave them in messes on the floor at the end of the night," I say. "No more keeping yourself back from me. I need all of you."

"Jesus," he rasps, his voice thick with emotion. He presses into me, so close I feel his heart pounding against my chest, beating as fast as mine. "You want me to make love to you, little one?"

"So bad." I clench my hands on his shoulders, tugging helplessly at his shirt as desire spikes higher, rising more swiftly than before. The need to feel his weight on top of me, to feel him inside me... God, I'm going to lose my mind if he isn't mine soon. I need him. Here and now. Like I've never needed anything before.

"You're beautiful," he says, his eyes dark obsidian. And oh, I know that look, the one that hints at every wicked thing he wants to do to me. It promises pleasure I've only dreamed about.

Heat twists in my belly at the sight of it, spreading outward in ever-widening ripples. I nearly cry at the sight of it. He's done telling me no. *Finally.*

My gaze falls to his lips, eager for more of his kisses. Will they be tinged with the truth now? Will love change the taste of his lips and the shape of his tongue? I moan at the thought, dying to know. I want to know everything about this man. Everything.

"Catriona," he breathes, his voice husky, and then his mouth descends on mine. His tongue darts out, licking at the seam of my lips. He backs me toward the windows, teasing his tongue across my bottom lip at the same time.

My back hits the cool glass, pulling a moan from my lips. It feels good against my overheated skin, the dichotomy of sensations overwhelming. Andreas reaches for my hands, pulling them up above my head to pin them against the glass. The move leaves me trapped beneath him, completely at his mercy. I like it far too much.

"Oh," I whisper, a shock of desire ripping through me.

He swoops, claiming my mouth, possessing it. He's not sweet and gentle this time. He's all dark and wicked, taking what belongs to him. And God, I love every minute of it. His tongue surges into my mouth, playing with mine until I'm weak in the knees and trembling. Somehow, he unmakes me and puts me back together at the same time, forging me into some new being. I'm not poor little Catriona Grady in this moment. I'm something bigger, bolder, a woman worthy of devotion.

He bites my bottom lip, pulling it into his mouth to suck on it.

Something inside rises hot and fast, wanting him as crazy as he's making me. So I bite his lip. I suck on it. I tease him too. He growls my name, his patience and composure scattering. Our tongues dance together, growing more urgent, more desperate.

We break apart gasping for air, gulping it greedily into lungs starving for oxygen. It doesn't slow him down any. He moves to my neck, nipping and biting the sensitive flesh beneath my ear, raking his teeth across it.

I cry out in bliss. And then lose my breath when his rough hands glide down my body, gathering the hem of my dress in his hands.

"I want to eat you right here while you watch the city below," he rasps, his eyes gleaming with greedy desire. "Are you going to let me?"

"Yes," I sob. Something about the possibility of being caught excites me, making me desperate to give him exactly what he wants. No, *I* want it. I want him to eat me here and now, with all of Houston on the other side of the glass. I don't care who sees us. A naughty little part of me hopes they do see. I hope they do catch us. I want the whole world to know that I belong to this man and this man alone.

"Good girl," he croons, the vibrations of his words sending another wave of desire through me. The way he says those two words... Lord, I think I'd walk through fire just to hear him call me a good girl in that sinful whiskey and smoke voice.

He presses a kiss to my throat and then slowly works my dress up my body. The cool air kisses my skin, making me sob his name in anticipation. He releases my hands long enough to pull the dress off over my head and drop it on the floor, leaving me in nothing but my torn panties.

"Goddamn," he growls, his eyes raking like wildfire over me. His hands clench and unclench as if he's fighting to keep them off me. "You aren't wearing a bra."

"It's built into the dress."

"Lucky dress," he says, taking a step back. His gaze sweeps down my body, taking in every inch of me. I love the way he looks at me as if he's never seen anything more beautiful. I'm full of flaws and imperfections. My body looks nothing like his. But when he looks at me, I feel like a priceless work of art because I know that's what he sees. It's written all over his face.

"I don't know where to start with you," he murmurs.

"Touch me," I plead, not above begging.

He reaches out, brushing one thumb across my nipple.

I gasp in pleasure, arching forward for more as my arms tremble and fall to my sides.

Andreas makes a small sound in the back of his throat and gently lifts them back over my head. "Keep them up, little one," he says. "I don't want you rushing me or touching what's mine. We both know you can't help yourself."

I whimper because he's right. He turns me into someone else, someone desperate and needy. I'm greedy with him, impatient and willing to be a little bit naughty to get what I want. When I'm with him, I'm so wrapped in desire, even the air caresses my body, teasing and taunting me, making me burn hotter, making me need him more.

My eyes fall closed as he touches me again, slowly tormenting me with soft passes over my nipples. It feels so damn good. I arch and mewl beneath him, aching for more. But Andreas takes his time and makes me take mine. He lets the anticipation build until I feel like I'm going to shatter apart.

"Oh!" I cry out, my knees buckling when he dips his head, his mouth covering one breast. He wedges his knee between my legs, holding me up against the window with his body. His tongue wraps around my nipple and then his teeth.

I sob his name, writhing in bliss.

He moves from breast to breast, biting and kissing until I'm dizzy with pleasure. It liquefies my insides, reforms me into something new. And then he starts a slow descent down my body. His wicked lips touch me everywhere, lavishing attention on my body. By the time he drops to his knees, I'm a sobbing, babbling mess.

He slips my torn panties down my legs, carefully lifting one foot and then the other to pull them from my body. Instead of placing my left leg back on the ground, he presses his lips to my inner thigh and drapes it over his broad shoulder.

"Oh, little one," he breathes, tracing my soaked lips with one finger. He drags it down my slit, almost like he's petting me right there. He's staring at my pussy, pure reverence stamped across his face.

I squirm in embarrassment. In ecstasy. In need. I hardly know which I feel more. But I watch in spellbound silence as he brings his finger to his lips and sucks it clean, those onyx eyes pure black and glittering with lust.

"I need you," he rasps, his voice hoarse. "Now. Fuck, little one. I need you."

"Then take me, Andreas," I whisper, shifting position to maintain my balance as he leans closer, his dark head bent.

"God, rabbit," he groans, his breath blowing hot against my pussy. "You've got the prettiest pussy. I don't know how I've stayed out of it this long." His gaze flickers up to mine, his obsidian eyes locking with mine. He holds my gaze captive as he flicks his tongue out, taking one long lick of me from top to bottom.

That first taste does something to him...and something to me. My stomach muscles clench, a wave of pleasure unlike anything I've ever felt hitting me. It's so strong, so good. I know immediately that I'll never be the same again.

He growls—a savage, feral sound that vibrates against my core. Patient Andreas disappears between one heartbeat and the next. Wicked, wanton Andreas snatches control away, wresting it from his grasp with ease. He presses me back against the windows, spreads me wide...and devours me. His mouth is everywhere, his lips and teeth and tongue touching every part of me. One minute, he's playing with my clit, the next, he's fucking me with it.

My hands slip on the glass, my sobs echoing around the room. He's the only thing keeping me upright. My legs lost the ability to hold me as soon as he started eating me. I can't even *feel* my legs.

"Andreas, Andreas," I chant as he sends me barreling toward an orgasm.

He feels it coming and growls, backing off.

I cry out in disappointment, but he's not finished with me yet.

He spins me around, plastering my body up against the glass. "Let the city see you, little one," he breathes, spreading my legs, angling my hips...positioning me just so. "Let everyone who looks to the heavens watch a goddess shine."

He spreads my cheeks this time, making me gasp and stutter. It's so dirty, so naughty. So...perfect. He eats me from behind, loud and messy. I writhe against the windows, pushing back against his face, sobbing his name. My reflection bounces back to me, my blonde hair all wild, my eyes so dilated they're almost black. I look wanton and wild, so unlike the timid girl I was before I met him. I'm not that girl anymore. I'm someone else. I'm *his*.

The city reflects like stars below us, thousands of lights trapped in the glass. Cars pass in an endless, silent stream. Do they see us? Do they know how much I love this man? Probably not. If they notice us at all, they probably think we're just two horny people doing the deed. They have no idea that my heart beats for him, that I breathe for him.

"Goddamn, rabbit," he growls, slipping his hand between my legs to play with my clit. He bites my right cheek and then runs his nose up the crevice of my ass. "I want to take my dick out, bend you over the couch, and fuck this little hole until you're screaming for me."

"Andreas," I moan, my core clenching.

"You'd let me, wouldn't you?" he asks.

"Y-yes," I sob. I'd let him do anything he wanted, and I'd love it. Because that's what he does to me. Nothing feels wrong or forbidden or dirty with him. It all feels so damn right.

"Good girl," he breathes. This time, his tongue replaces his nose. He touches it to my back entrance, eating me there as his thumb runs in circles around my clit.

I sob his name, pressing back against him, trying to get closer, silently pleading for more. I'm close. So close. He works two fingers inside of me, slowly stretching me. I writhe, so tangled in bliss, I'm not sure how this is even real. Every part of me tingles and hums.

He curls his fingers up, stroking that same spot he found in the car earlier. His tongue teases my back entrance. His thumb jiggles my clit. All three sensations crash together, melting me from the inside out. I shout his name, my orgasm knocking me off my feet.

He catches me in his arms, lowering me to the rug. He spreads me out, and devours me all over again, eating me until I'm begging for mercy because my clit is so sensitive every lick has me ready to catapult out of my skin. Each touch has a sob pouring from my lips.

He delivers a final open-mouthed kiss to my clit, one so damn scorching hot, he sends me into another orgasm. It's all lips and tongue, and intimate, erotic possession. I ride out the waves, grasping at the thick fibers of the rug as if that's going to tether me to reality.

"I love you," he whispers, scooping me up into his arms. "God, I love you, little one."

"Andreas," I breathe, curling into him, too boneless to do much else.

He carries me through the penthouse, which passes in blurs. I see nothing until he lays me out in the middle of a giant bed under a glass ceiling. Silvery clouds paint the sky, light pollution hiding the stars. I tip my head forward, searching for him.

I find him watching me with those bedroom eyes, barely contained need and reverent devotion stamped across every line of his face as he undresses slowly. He's so damn beautiful, like a sleek, dangerous panther. He's powerful and strong, not because he's a billionaire or successful or beautiful or any of those things. But because of who *he* is. He is unshakable.

I love that about him.

"Spread your legs, rabbit," he orders, his voice gritty as he pulls his dress shirt off and tosses it over the foot of the bed. "Let me see heaven while I undress."

I shyly spread them, letting him look his fill. I never knew that men liked to look at us down there so much, but this one certainly seems to enjoy it. Who am I to ruin his fun?

"Part your lips," he says. "Let me see it all."

"Andreas," I groan.

"Now, little one."

I huff out a breath and then slowly slip my hand between my legs, spreading my lower lips for him. He grunts, squeezing his erection through his pants. That doesn't seem to satisfy him because he quickly reaches for the button, undoing it.

I moan when he releases the zipper and then pulls his cock out. He's so hard. With the overhead lights on, he's even bigger than he was by lamplight last night. I have no idea how he's going to fit inside me. But I'm ready to find out.

He strokes himself a few times, staring at my center. And then he curses and quickly finishes undressing. "I need in you," he growls, climbing onto the bed with me. He prowls over me, leaning down to capture my mouth in a searing kiss.

I taste myself on his lips and gasp. He eases my hand from between my legs, fitting his body between them. He locks our fingers together, pulling my hand up over my head as he deepens the kiss. Our mouths work together, his kiss hungry and demanding, as if he's starving for me.

"Are you sure you're ready for me, Catriona?" he asks, pulling my leg up over his waist. His erection glides through my folds, the broad head grinding against my clit. "Once I'm in you, I'm not letting you go, little one."

"Andreas?" I tip my head back, looking up at him. "Stop talking and make love to me."

"Bossy," he chuckles.

"I'm not bossy. I'm practicing."

"Yeah?" He grins at me. "What are you practicing, rabbit?"

"Being successful."

His grin widens, his expression soft and warm. "You planning for a future of bossing me around, rabbit?"

"No." I shake my head against the pillow, holding his gaze. "I'm planning for a future of loving you and letting you love me, Andreas."

"Fuck," he breathes, heat flaring in his eyes. He tips his head, taking my lips in a hot kiss. By the time he lets me up for air, we're both panting. We don't talk after that. There's nothing left to say.

He notches his erection at my entrance and slowly presses forward.

I watch his, fascinated by his expression. It's so beautiful to me. His eyes blaze with heat. His bottom lip is caught between his teeth. His cheeks are flushed with desire. He focuses intently on not hurting me, but the intense look of pleasure on his face as he slowly pushes into me lets me know he's in heaven.

At first, I feel stretched and full. But then the stretch turns into a burn that grows in intensity. A moment later, a sharp pain burns through me as my virgin barrier tears. It's intense enough to bring tears to my eyes. But even as I tense up, it begins to dull and fade.

"I'm sorry, little one," Andreas whispers, resting his forehead against mine. "I'm so sorry."

"I'm okay," I promise.

"You're crying."

"I'm happy," I whisper, clinging to him as tears course down my cheeks. "I'm s-so happy, Andreas." Even though it hurts a little, that's not what I feel. All I feel is awe and joy and happiness. For the first time in my life, I know what it is to be complete. I know what it is to belong. This right here is where I fit. It's where I'm meant to be.

"Little one," he breathes, brushing my tears away with his thumbs. "I love you."

I sob his name in response.

He surges forward, burying himself inside me completely. We both fall still, marveling in this moment. He shudders on top of me, groaning my name. I cry out as he pivots his hips and pulls back, sliding out slowly before he sheathes himself inside me again. Waves of pleasure flow through me, knocking me breathless.

He links our hands together above my head, keeping his weight from crushing me with one knee planted on the bed. Our bodies slide together, his so much harder than mine. Mine yields to his, submitting to him.

"God, Catriona," he groans, rocking into me in slow drives. "You feel so fucking good, little one. I may keep you on my cock all night. Think you can take it?"

"Yes. No. Yes. Andreas," I whine, not sure I know how to answer that question.

He chuckles quietly, running his nose up the side of my face. "You can take it, rabbit." He nips my ear and then the pulse hammering beneath my jaw. "You can take anything I give you." He pulls back until the head of his cock teases at my entrance and then thrusts forward harder than before.

A keening cry erupts from my lips, my body bowing beneath his.

He does it again. And then a third time.

"See? You were made to fuck, Catriona." He leaves a trail of kisses all over my throat, driving me crazy as he circles his hips, grinding the root of his erection against my clit with each ridiculously slow thrust. "And I was made to please you."

"Please," I sob, my womb clenching, aching. I need... "More."

"Fuck, little one. You want it harder?"

"Yes!"

He pulls back and thrusts again, a powerful strike of his hips that has me seeing stars. "Like this, Catriona? Is this how you want it?" He does it again, stealing my breath this time.

"Yes, yes," I sob, wailing the word into the room.

"Take it then, rabbit," he growls, claiming my mouth in a deep kiss. He fucks me hard, each deep thrust sending me reeling further and further into orbit. His skin slaps against mine, filling the room with our sounds.

"Christ, I love the way you feel," he grunts against my lips. "I love how sweet you sound. I love the way you smell and how good you taste." He plays with my tongue for a minute before backing off. "By the time you leave this bed tomorrow, you'll be dripping my cum." He dips his head, pressing his lips to my ear. "If I'm lucky, you'll be pregnant with my kid."

"Andreas," I moan, my inner muscles clamping down around him.

"Oh, rabbit," he says, his tone absolutely wicked. "You want me to breed you, don't you?"

"I...I..."

"Is that why you let me in you without a condom, Catriona? You want me to breed you?" He drives his cock into me again, and then retreats to start the electric glide all over again. It unravels me, leaves me mindless, boneless. He takes me hard, holding nothing back. And I can't hold back either.

"Yes," I whisper, trailing open-mouthed kisses all over his chest and shoulders. "I want it, Andreas. So damn bad." I've wanted it ever since he mentioned it the day we met. A big family, a loving home. That's my big dream for the future. That's success to me. That's what I want more than anything. I want to be a wife and a mom and spoil the people in my life with affection and love and all the things I missed growing up.

"Then come for me," he orders me, releasing my hands to grasp my hips. "Give me one more perfect moment to add to my list." He lifts me into each powerful thrust, hitting spots inside that leave me gasping beneath him.

Heat coils in my belly, rippling outward. I cry out his name, trying to warn him that I'm there. But he doesn't need the warning. He already knows my body better than I do. As soon as the orgasm creeps up on me, he pulls my leg up over his shoulder and pounds into me, hitting one spot again and again with ruthless precision.

I claw down his shoulders.

"Catriona!" he shouts in bliss. "I love you."

Those three words on his lips are all it takes to send me over the edge. I scream soundlessly as I fly apart, coming hard. My vision goes black, sound fades. Shattering bliss rolls through me in waves of eternity. He follows me over the edge with a wordless roar. His body goes taut above me, his muscles locked in ecstasy. His cum spills into me, splashing warm against my womb.

When it's over, he falls against me, rolling to the side to keep from crushing me beneath him. He pulls me into his arms, breathing hard. I cuddle up against his sweaty chest, listening to his heart pounding beneath my ear.

"Andreas? What are your perfect moments?"

"The moment I met you," he murmurs, pulling the blankets up over us. "The first time I kissed you. The moment I woke up with you in my arms. Watching you come. At the stadium when you smiled up at me and stole every last piece of my heart. The moment at dinner when I realized you love me to." His hand drifts down my side. "This moment."

"Oh," I whisper, my heart expanding in my chest. "Those are my moments too." I pause. "Well, mine is watching you come, not watching me come."

"Trust me, little one," he laughs quietly. "If you could see yourself come, it'd be your favorite moment too."

"Whatever," I mumble, rolling my eyes. Trying to, anyway. They're too heavy to open. "Don't be crazy."

"I passed crazy a week again, Catriona. Right about the time I met you."

I snort, pretty sure he passed crazy way before then. But I'm tired so I don't tell him that.

Chapter Nine

Andreas

"We are not having sex right now, Andreas Romano," Catriona shouts, darting around the island away from me. "I'm busy trying to learn things!"

Three days ago, she decided she wanted to learn everything there is to learn about Romano International. I brought her home a bunch of old articles and press releases and historical documents about the company. She spends part of every day going through them, peppering me with questions no one alive knows the damn answers to. She doesn't like that much.

It's been a little over a week since Houston, and everything has been fucking perfect between us. Better than that. I never imagined my life could be a goddamn fairytale, but if ever a woman could make friends with birds and breathe magic into the world, it's Catriona. She's certainly breathed magic into my world. Every day with her is better than the last.

I grin and prowl toward her. "Good. You can learn how to sit on the island like a good girl and let me eat you for dessert," I say.

"I..." She pauses, thinking about it. And then she quickly shakes her head and darts around the other side of the island. "No way. Autumn almost caught us in the living room last night. You have to keep your hands to yourself outside of the bedroom."

"Uh, fuck no."

"Uh, heck yes," she says, making me chuckle.

"Have you ever said a curse word in your life, rabbit?"

"I say curse words."

"Yeah?" I stop chasing after her and lean up against the counter, crossing my arms. I'm dying to hear this. "Like what?"

"Damn and hell," she says.

A grin overtakes my face as her chin comes up, her nose shooting into the air in a haughty display. She's too goddamn cute. I'm not even going to tell her those don't even fucking count as curse words.

"Come here and kiss me," I say and then curse when my phone immediately rings.

She smirks at me, scooping her shit up off the island and darting out of the kitchen before I can get my hands on her. That's all right though. I already know exactly where she's going.

I pull my phone out of my pocket, frowning when I see Cash's number on the screen. We haven't talked much lately. I'm not sure if he's avoiding me or if I'm avoiding him. Maybe a little bit of both. He's still pissed Giant and I went sniffing around Copper Creek. And I'm not looking forward to telling him about Catriona.

I'm not ashamed of her in the least. I'll fight for her against all comers. But he's already been through hell because of my father's involvement with his company. And Catriona's brother ordered the attack on his pregnant wife. The only reason she's safe is because they fucked up and got her twin instead. He's got enough stress on his plate right now.

But I've put it off for long enough already.

I swipe to answer.

"Hey, brother," I murmur, putting the phone to my ear.

"Hey," he says. "We need you at the clubhouse. Emergency meeting."

"Shit. What's going on?"

"Cowboy found a fucking note on his door," he growls. "Looks like Brady left it there." Brady is our former piece of shit prospect. He caused us nothing but grief before he sold some information to the Vipers and then disappeared on us. We hoped he'd stay gone. Apparently not. "They're threatening to come after our women."

"Jesus Christ," I breathe.

"Do me a favor?"

"Whatever you need."

"Don't take this the wrong way, brother," he says, his voice soft. "But you might want to think about leaving Catriona at home tonight. Cowboy's mad as hell. Hands will be too. I don't want her to overhear anything that she takes the wrong way."

I pause for a long moment, staring blankly at the porcelain countertop.

"You know," I finally say.

Cash snorts. "You've known me for how fucking long? Of course I fucking know about her, jackass. I've just been waiting for you to nut up and tell me."

"It's not like that," I say. "I'm not trying to hide her. I plan to marry this girl. But she's been through hell. I'm trying to introduce her to everyone slowly." I expel a breath. "And I didn't want to stress you the fuck out when you have twins on the way."

He laughs abruptly. "Motherfucker, I have twins on the way. I'm already stressed the fuck out." He sobers. "But I get it. Ain't saying I like you keeping shit from me, but I get it. This last year has been fucked, but we're making it, brother. We'll make it through this shit and whatever comes next too. We always do."

"Yeah," I sigh. "You think Cowboy or Hands will be a problem?"

"Nah," he says. "Cowboy won't hold her responsible for her fucking dumbass brother, and Hands is worried about Samara and Scout, but the Vipers have nothing to do with them. I just don't want anyone to say something in the heat of the moment and hurt her feelings. Emotions are running high right now. When she meets everyone, it shouldn't be in the midst of this bullshit, you feel me?"

"Yeah, I feel you," I say, drumming my fingers on the island. I'm not keen on introducing her to everyone in the midst of this new issue either. Seeing them worried will only make her feel worse, and that's the last thing I want. None of this is her fault. It's on her fucking brother and his MC. This is their doing, not hers. "I'll be there."

"See you, brother."

I disconnect and then call Autumn, who is supposed to be meeting with a lawyer about Jimmy Gatlin. I offered to go with her, but she refused to let me. Apparently, she's a big girl now and doesn't need her brother bullying people into doing things her way. Whatever the fuck that means.

"Hey. I'm running late," she says, out of breath when she answers on the second ring. "The meeting with this lawyer ran over. I'll be leaving soon."

"I need you to come straight home." I exit the kitchen, headed toward my office at the back of the house. Catriona loves curling up on the sofa in there to read while I work at my desk at night. Neither of us ever gets much done. We spend the whole damn time stealing glances at each other. Eventually, she puts her work aside and crawls into my lap, or I put my laptop aside and crawl onto the couch with her. I've fucked her raw in my office. "Something came up and I need to head out for a while. Catriona will be here alone."

"Oh." I hear the frown in Autumn's voice. "Is everything okay?"

"Not sure," I admit, not lying to her. I don't want to frighten her, but this involves her too. She's my sister. That means she has a target on her back too. "The Hell's Vipers are threatening to come after our people again. I need you to take this serious, Autumn. They're dangerous."

"I know," she whispers. "I'll be careful, Andreas."

"Can you wait with Catriona until I get home?"

"You aren't going to do anything stupid, are you?"

"No, of course not. I'm just going to the clubhouse to help make sure everyone has security in place and our families are all protected," I explain, stepping into the hallway. The light is on at the end of the hall, letting me know I was right. Catriona is in my office. It's her favorite room in the house.

Autumn expels a relieved breath. "Okay. I'll tell this crazy man that I need to leave," she says. "He's driving me insane anyway. Why didn't you tell me Jason had a brother? And why is he so...*ugh*?"

"You're meeting with Zane?" I ask, arching a brow. Zane Montoya just moved to town not long ago. I don't know him well, but he's a good guy. I can see him driving Autumn crazy though. He's calm, controlled. She's a little like a hurricane.

"Aha! So you do know him!" she cries. "You could have warned me about him."

"You... Just hurry up," I say, refusing to have this argument. I already know I won't win. It's impossible to win this argument. We've been having a variation of it since she was old enough to talk, and it always ends with her verbally kicking my ass. If anyone should have been a lawyer, she should have.

"Be careful, Andreas."

"I will. Come straight home." I disconnect and then slip my phone into my pocket before ducking into my office.

"Did you know Romano International used to have an entire pirate crew on the payroll?" she asks, lifting her head to look at me over the back of the couch. "When the company first started in the 1800s, your great great great great great great great great great" –she takes a dramatic breath— "great great great great great great grandfather hired a band of pirates to defend his ships as they were carrying cargo from Italy to the West Indies."

"That's way too many greats, little one," I say, smiling at her.

"Close enough," she mumbles. "My point is: your grandpa was so cool."

"The Italian government didn't agree," I chuckle. "He was heavily fined for conspiring with pirates and nearly lost the company."

"Well, that's lame."

I shake my head, strolling toward her. Once I reach her, I kneel in front of the couch, taking the book from her hands and setting it aside with her place saved so she can pick it back up later. "I have to leave for a little while," I murmur, linking our fingers together and bringing them to my lips to press a kiss to her knuckles. "I need to go to the clubhouse."

"Oh. Um, is everything okay?"

"It will be," I promise, tucking strands of hair behind her ears. "The Vipers are causing problems."

"Oh no," she whispers, her expression falling. "Because of me?"

"No. This has nothing to do with you. As far as I know, your brother still doesn't know you're here," I say, holding her gaze so she knows I'm not lying to her. "They're angry with me because I cut them off financially. That's not on you."

"What...what kind of problem is it?" she asks, her gaze flickering across my face.

I hesitate for a moment.

"Please tell me," she whispers. "The truth may upset me, but I'm strong enough to handle it, Andreas. Please don't treat me like I'm not. Please don't leave me in the dark about things that impact my life too. I've spent five years living that way already."

"Fuck," I growl. "They're threatening to come after our people again, rabbit. After our women."

Her eyes fall closed, a sad sigh rippling across the space between us. "Connor," she says. "He's really doing it again."

"It looks that way," I murmur, wishing like hell that wasn't the case. Wishing like hell I didn't have to tell her this. She loves her brother fiercely, and he just keeps breaking her heart. She deserves so much better. It fucking kills me that he's too goddamn selfish to give it to her. "I'm sorry, little one."

"Me too," she sighs.

I scoop her up into my arms, holding her close to my heart for a long moment. She burrows into me, clinging like a little koala bear, her face pressed to my throat. She's quiet in my arms, far too quiet. I don't want to leave her like this.

"You should go," she says after a moment, pulling back. "Your brothers need you."

"So do you."

She gives me a wobbly smile. "Right now, they need you to help make sure everyone is safe," she says. "Once you're done with that, you can hold me all night. I'll be okay until then."

"Are you sure?" I ask, reluctant to leave her here alone.

"I'm positive." She tips her face up to mine. "Kiss me, Andreas Romano. And then go help your brothers protect our family."

"Our family?"

She gives me a little smile. "I'm kind of hoping they'll want to keep me."

"Oh, we're keeping you," I murmur, claiming her lips in a heated kiss.

The meeting at the clubhouse goes about how I expected it would. My brothers are pissed. Even those without women to protect are livid. They want to load up and ride for

Copper Creek to solve this shit now, but Cash talks everyone down. We decide to keep everyone at the clubhouse for the next few days and beef up security.

The girls handle the news better than anyone else. Then again, women usually do. We spend so much time trying to protect them, we tend to forget that they're a hell of a lot stronger than we give them credit for. God knows, Catriona is one of the strongest people I know.

While the girls coo over Scout and Gloria and Rulie—the couple who help run the clubhouse for us—keep an eye on them, I pull my brothers aside for a discussion. Bender is still on tour and Damien "Angel" De Angelis is still in Belldonia, but everyone else is here. There's no time like the present to let them know about Catriona.

"I won't be staying here," I tell everyone.

"Uh, what the fuck?" Rafe "Lynch" Soracco bitches from his seat at the bar. "This is an all-hands-on-deck situation, motherfucker. You don't just get to opt-out."

"What Lynch said," Hands complains, scowling at me. He looks like he hasn't been sleeping much, but there's a lightness in his eyes that never really leaves since he claimed Samara. He's happier than I've ever seen him. "I'm moving my little girl in until this shit blows over. She doesn't need to be exposed to you assholes and your germs, but this is the safest place for her, so I'm taking a calculated risk. You aren't special. Pack your shit. You're staying too."

"I can't," I say quietly, glancing at him and then at Cowboy. "I've got Autumn staying with me." I pause. "And Catriona Grady."

"Say that again," Cowboy drawls, his blue eyes hard.

"Catriona Grady has been living with me for the last week and a half," I say quietly, meeting his gaze. "Before you get all pissy about it, you should know she moved in because she found out what the Hell's Vipers did to Kyra and left home. You should also know that she's going to be my wife so anything you say about her, you say about me."

Cowboy stares me down for a long moment and then huffs out a curse. "Jesus fucking Christ," he growls. "Did you plan on telling us?"

"I knew," Fifth says.

"Knew all along," Giant rumbles, reaching over the bar to grab a beer. He hands one to Lynch too. Lynch immediately pops the top and takes a pull, opting not to get involved in this argument. He chooses his battles wisely.

"Bender met her a week ago," I say.

"He wasn't hiding it, Cowboy," Cash murmurs, playing peacekeeper.

I appreciate the hell out of him for backing me up even though I didn't tell him myself. And I don't blame Cowboy for being pissed that I haven't said anything to him either. It was a dick a move, but I wasn't trying to keep her a secret from him.

"Her brother doesn't know she's with me," I explain. "And we're not sure if she's going to be scooped up in this bust or not. She's scared, and all she knows of us is the bullshit she's heard from them. I'm trying to juggle fifteen different balls to undo the damage they've done to her. She's been my priority. Until she's safe, she'll be my priority. That's where my head is. That's what I was thinking about. It wasn't about you, brother."

Cowboy pulls his hat off and rakes a hand through his hair. He expels a sharp breath and then shakes his head. "Fuck," he finally says, his rigid stance loosening. "I'm not mad at you, brother. Just surprised. Secrets don't make friends, motherfucker."

"Noted," I say, a ghost of a smile on my lips.

He smirks at me and then sobers. "She's scared of us, huh?"

"Nah, she likes me," Giant says, grinning. "It's the rest of you shady assholes she doesn't trust."

"Man, fuck you." Fifth flips him off. "You're the worst out of all of us."

"True story," Hacker agrees from his spot against the wall near the bar.

Lynch and Cowboy chime in with their agreement.

"Would you all shut the fuck up?" Cash growls, shaking his dark head. "Jesus. We haven't even been here an hour and I'm already hating my fucking life. Playboy, get back to your girl. We'll take turns helping you keep an eye on her until this shit blows over. It'll give her a chance to get used to us one on one, and it'll give her a little more protection in case they've figured out she's here." He eyes each of my brothers, his expression serious. "She's one of us now. If they come for her, they aren't leaving with her unless it's her choice."

"Agreed," Giant says without hesitation.

"Agreed," Fifth echoes.

One by one, every single one of my brothers in the room echoes their agreement, throwing their allegiance behind Catriona. They'll fight for her. They'll bleed for her if that's what it takes. She's mine now, and that makes her one of theirs too.

"Thank you," I rasp, gratitude coursing through me.

Cash smacks me on the back.

I say my goodbyes and head out, eager to get back to Catriona and Autumn. I don't want them home alone any longer than necessary until this shit blows over. If the Vipers are coming for our families, they aren't going to get them. Not today or any other day. Not without a fight. We may not be outlaws or criminals, but we protect what's ours.

"I'm on my way," I say fifteen minutes later, pulling my bike to the side of the road when Autumn calls. "I'll be there in ten."

"Is Catriona with you?" she asks.

"What do you mean is she with me?" I growl, my blood running cold.

"It took me longer to get here than I thought it would," she rushes to say. "I checked the entire house, but I couldn't find her anywhere. So I looked in the garage. Her car isn't here, Andreas. Did she go with you to the clubhouse?"

My heart stops beating. It just fucking...stops.

"No," I rasp, my hand numb around the phone. "No, she didn't go with me."

"Andreas," Autumn whispers, genuine fear in her voice.

"I know," I grit out, the same emotion running through me in a current. If she isn't with me and she isn't at the house, there are only so many places she could be. After finding out not even two hours ago that the Vipers are threatening to come after Hadley, Samara, and Kyra, that list of options narrows significantly.

She went back to Copper Creek.

She went to see her brother.

Fuck, little one. What are you doing?

"Stay inside and lock the doors," I order Autumn. "I'm going after her."

"Please be careful," Autumn pleads. "I need you to come home, Andreas. You're my brother and I need you to come home, okay?"

"I'm coming home, baby sister," I promise, my voice soft.

"Okay," she sniffles. "Please bring Catriona home too."

"Plan on it," I growl. "Stay inside."

"Okay."

I hang up and then immediately dial Giant.

"What's up, fucker?"

"Catriona went to confront her brother," I tell him.

"Shit," he growls, sobering. "How long ago?"

"I don't know, but I'm going after her," I say.

"Let's ride."

"I'm not asking."

"Good, because we're ride or die, motherfucker. You don't have to ask. We ride until we die, period. We're going to get your girl," he says. "Where are you?"

I check the road signs and give him my location.

"Be there in five."

"Just you, Giant," I say quietly. "If you bring everyone..."

"Yeah, I know. It'll turn into a fucking war."

Chapter Ten

Catriona

My brother's house sits at the end of a cul-de-sac in a dying neighborhood in Copper Creek. The gray two-story Cape Cod-style house is in good condition, but it looks sad and lonely. The houses on either side have for sale signs hanging in the front yards. They've been on the market for a while but living next to a known biker hangout isn't appealing to most buyers. Neither is buying real estate in a town where most people live below the poverty line and job opportunities are scarce.

A light shines in the front window and my brother's bike is parked in the driveway. Thankfully, his is the only one tonight. I didn't come here to talk to the Vipers. I came to talk to Connor. Andreas is going to be mad at me when he finds out, but I have to do this.

I've been putting it off for long enough already.

I don't know if I can stop Connor from doing whatever it is he and the Vipers are planning to do, but I owe it to Andreas to try. I owe it to myself to try too. If I don't, I'll always wonder if I could have stopped them. I'll always wonder if I could have made a difference.

For a long time, I kept my mouth shut and watched my brother slip further and further down a dark path. I can't do that this time. Ignorance isn't bliss, and I know that now. I think I've always known that, but I was always too afraid to rock the boat. I didn't want to lose the only family I had left. Connor is my brother and I love him. I'll always love him. But loving someone doesn't mean enabling them. It doesn't mean supporting them even when they're destroying themselves. Sometimes, loving someone means loving them enough to walk away.

If I have to make a choice between family and forever...I choose forever.

I choose Andreas.

I pull into the driveway and park. My hands shake as I kill the engine and climb out. It feels like a lifetime since I left here. Part of me feels guilty for cutting off all contact with Connor like I did, but I think I needed to do it. Had I not, he would have badgered me into coming home and I probably would have let him. He's my brother. I *hate* fighting with him.

Part of me will always feel like I owe him because he raised me. But I don't owe him my peace of mind. I don't owe him my future and my happiness. I can't spend the rest of my life trying to straighten his out for him.

I push my car door closed and jog up the steps to the front door, and then I hesitate. Should I knock? Use my key? I'm not sure. This isn't my home anymore. It hasn't felt like home to me in a very long time.

Before I can figure out if I should knock or just go in, Connor pulls open the door. His green eyes run over me. Relief blooms in their depths before he quickly masks it.

"Catriona," he growls, blocking the door with his body. He looks tired. His eyes are bruised beneath as if he hasn't been sleeping much. His jaw is scruffy where he hasn't shaved, his hair mussed. His black t-shirt is fresh and clean, but his jeans have a hole in the knee and grease down one leg.

"Um, hi," I whisper, fidgeting nervously.

"Why are you here?"

Okay, wow. That's not exactly the reaction I was expecting from him.

"I came to talk," I say, frowning. He seems so...hostile. Like I did something wrong.

He stares at me for a long moment, the silence between us tense and strained, his gaze unwavering. "Your note said it all, Catriona. We don't need to rehash the shit now."

I gape at him. "Do you even care where I've been for the last week and a half, Connor?"

"You said you were with a friend." He shrugs.

I open my mouth and then snap it closed, my temper rising.

What is wrong with him? Where is my brother, the one who told DHS that they'd have to call the National Guard to separate us because he wasn't going to let them take me from him no matter what? The one who went to court and fought to keep me because I was his family and I belonged with him, not with some stranger I didn't know? Where's the guy who used to sit in my room when I had nightmares and came home with eight different kinds of feminine pads when I had my first period because he panicked and didn't know what to buy?

The guy standing before me isn't that one. Because that guy would never have let me leave for a week without knowing where I was and who I was with. He would have lost his dang mind trying to find me. This guy...this one isn't one I want to know.

"You're a liar, Connor Grady," I say, seething in fury. And maybe a little bit of sadness too. "My whole life you told me that I could always count on you, but that was a lie. The only person who can count on you is you. You're a selfish bully and a criminal. You lie and cheat and steal and hurt people and you do it because you like to do it. You're not a good person."

He stares at me, not saying anything. Not reacting at all.

"You lied about the Silver Spoon MC too," I shout at him, waving my hands like a crazy person. I don't even care if the few neighbors left on the block hear me. I don't care if the whole stupid town hears me. "They aren't bad people. Andreas Romano is a better man than you'll ever be, Connor Grady! And just so you know, I'm marrying him." I glare at him, defiant and ferociously angry, just daring him to insult the man I love. "I've been living with him all week. Not that you care."

His jaw tics, but he still doesn't say anything.

"I know that you and the Vipers are planning to target their families. Do it and I'll tell them everything I know about the Vipers," I growl the warning, meaning every word. Andreas might not ask it of me, but I made my choice. To protect him and the people he loves, I'll spill all the Vipers' secrets. "You may think you kept me in the dark all this time, but you're wrong. I know a lot more than you think I do."

Connor eyes me for a minute. "You'd choose him over your own family?"

"I chose the family who chose me," I snap, glaring at him. "You chose the Vipers, Connor. Andreas chose me. Every single damn day since I met him, he's chosen me."

Connor opens his mouth to respond, but the roar of bikes in the distance silences him. He whips his head toward the end of the street and then looks back at me, something almost like panic in his gaze. "You need to leave before they find you here," he growls.

"I don't care about the stupid Vipers!" I cry, throwing my hands up.

"I do," he snaps. "Leave, Catriona. Now."

There's no reasoning with him, not when he doesn't want to see reason. He's made his choice, and I've made mine. My shoulders slump, the fight draining out of me.

"Go to hell, Connor Alaric Grady," I say, tears filling my eyes. I turn on my heel and start down the steps as two bikes roar around the corner. As soon as I catch sight of them, the tears fall faster. It's not the Vipers. It's Andreas and Giant. I'd recognize my man anywhere.

"Son of a bitch," Connor mutters behind me.

I draw to a stop at the bottom of the steps as Andreas and Giant race down the street toward us. I can tell by the look on Andreas's face that he's furious. His onyx eyes blaze with righteous fury. Every muscle in his body is rigid. He stops behind my car, his wild eyes running over me.

I stumble in his direction, my heart battered and bruised and a little bit broken.

"Are you okay, little one?" he asks, scooping me up into his arms. They close around me, holding me tight. His body trembles faintly, and I know I scared him. My tears fall faster, guilt rushing through me.

I silently shake my head, pressing my face to his throat.

"Did he hurt you?"

I shake my head again.

Andreas relaxes slightly, a little of the tension draining from him. "Let's get you home, rabbit," he murmurs in my ear. "Is there anything left here that you want to take?"

"Nothing," I whisper. Everything I need, I already have.

"Good. We're leaving your car," he says. "You're riding with me. I'm not letting you out of my sight again." He squeezes me in a hug and then presses his lips to my crown before tipping my head back. His eyes run over my face, his expression soft, full of worry. His thumbs run under my eyes, collecting my ears. "Be strong for me, rabbit. Just until we're home."

I take a deep breath, trying to get my emotions under control. He won't put me on the back of his bike until I do. No one protects me like Andreas. No one loves me like him. Choosing him wasn't a question. It wasn't a decision I had to make. I'll always choose him.

"Romano!" Connor shouts as he helps settle me onto the back of his bike and slips a helmet onto my head. "Get her the fuck out of here and don't let her come back."

"Grady!" Giant shouts back, lifting his middle fingers high in the sky. "You can't have her back, you ugly motherfucker. She's ours now."

Even though I feel like bawling, I leave my brother's house for the last time with a smile on my face.

"I'm so mad at you right now," Andreas whispers an hour later, trailing his hands up and down my arms as we cuddle in his giant bathtub. I'm seated in front of him, his body wrapped around me. He carried me up here as soon as we got home. He barely had the bike parked and I was crawling into his lap, sobbing.

"I'm not sorry," I say, leaning back against his chest. I tilt my head to the side, running my lips along the side of his jaw. "I had to try, Andreas. If there was even a chance that he'd listen to me, I had to take it."

"You told him about us," he says, tilting my head further back with his hand against my throat. His onyx eyes flicker across my face, searching.

"Of course I told him about you. I love you."

Pride flares in his eyes, darkening them. "What did he say?"

"Nothing." I frown at the reminder. "He didn't react at all. It was weird, Andreas."

"How so?"

"The only time he showed any emotion at all was when he heard the bikes and thought it was the MC. He panicked at the thought of them finding me there. The rest of the time he was just...a robot." I shrug helplessly, not sure how to explain. "It's like he wasn't my brother at all."

"I'm sorry, little one." Andreas dips his head, running his lips across my forehead. "I don't know what's going through his head or how he feels, but I do know what it's like to be a man who loves you beyond all reason, Catriona. He's losing you and even if he doesn't want to admit it, deep down, he knows that's his fault. That has to hurt like hell. It'd fucking destroy me, rabbit. Maybe this is his way of getting through it."

"Maybe." I sigh sadly. "I wish it didn't have to be this way."

"I know you do." He cuddles me closer, wrapping me all up in him. "Maybe someday it won't have to be. But for right now, you have to take care of you. You have to let *me* take care of you. Once the dust clears, we'll sort out the rest."

"Promise?"

"I promise," he whispers.

I turn around on his lap, sending water sloshing over the sides of the tub. He eyes me through slit lids as I straddle his hips, his hands settling around my waist. His hair his damp, sticking up all over the place. Somehow, it makes him look even more beautiful than ever.

"What are you doing?" he asks.

"Well," I say, leaning forward to wrap my arms around his neck. My hands play through the hair at the nape of his neck and then down the muscles of his shoulders and upper back. God, he's so strong. So fierce. "I've been thinking."

"Yeah?" A hint of a smile crosses his face. "What have you been thinking about, rabbit?"

"Your perfect moments," I say.

"Oh?" One brow arches.

"I'd like to add another one."

He grins, his eyes heating. "What does this one entail?"

I peep at him through my lashes, smiling shyly. I don't answer him though, not right away, at least. Instead, I lean forward and kiss his cheek and then his jaw. His throat and then his chest. I wiggle on his lap until his erection is right where I want it.

"Little one," he growls, his hands like vises around my waist.

I bite my lip to keep from laughing.

"Hmm?"

"Tell me what this moment entails," he orders me, all hot and bossy and completely perfect.

"Oh, nothing major," I tease, rolling my hips until his erection grinds against my clit. I fall forward against his chest, putting my mouth right up against his ear. "Just me asking you to marry me before you make love to me in the bathtub."

He growls my name.

I squeal, clinging to him as he stands in one fluid movement. Water sluices off us in a flood, soaking the floor around the tub. He steps out with me in his arms, without even missing a beat. He doesn't even stop to dry us off. He storms through the bathroom with me and then into the bedroom, tackling me onto the bed beneath him.

I squeal again, squirming as he pins me beneath him. Once he has me where he wants me, he reaches over my head, grabbing something out of his nightstand.

"Say it," he growls.

"But I wanted to ask in the bathtub," I tease.

"Say it, little one," he grits out.

"Fine!" I cry, giving in. "Andreas Christopher Romano, will you please marry me?"

"No."

I blink at him, shocked.

"That's not how this goes, rabbit," he says, his eyes soft. So damn soft I get lost in them. "You don't ask me to marry you. You don't ask me for anything. You tell me what you need, and I give it to you. That's how this thing between us works."

"Andreas," I whisper. He's so crazy. I love it so much.

"I'm the one who asks you, rabbit," he whispers, rubbing his nose along the side of mine. "I beg if that's what it takes to get you agree to become my wife. Marry me, little one. Make me the happiest goddamn man on this planet and tell me I can love you forever. Please."

"That's not a question."

He hitches my leg up over his hip with a soft growl, slipping inside me with one deep thrust. We both moan, clinging to one another. God, he feels so good. So damn good.

"Marry me, Catriona," he growls in my ear.

"Andreas."

"Marry me."

He nips my throat and then kisses my lips, making love to me so slowly I feel every ridge of his cock, feel every blissful drag against my inner walls. "Please, little one. I need you," he groans, writhing on top of me. "I'll always need you."

"Yes," I sob, unable to tease him any longer. "Yes, I'll marry you."

He falls still above me and then groans my name, shuddering.

"Andreas," I gasp when he slips a ring on my finger.

"You said you had to have a ring to marry me," he murmurs, bringing my hand up to his lips to kiss the solitaire princess cut diamond. The pride and devotion in his eyes sear me all the way to my bones and send me flying. With him, I'm always flying. And I never, ever want to come down.

I sob his name, this perfect, beautiful moment topping every single one that came before.

Epilogue

Andreas

<u>Five Years Later</u>

"Fuck, little one," I groan, writhing against the wall as Catriona takes me deep into her mouth before pulling back to start all over again. She tortures me, running her tongue along my shaft and humming in pleasure. Her small hand cups my balls, the nails of her other hand digging into my thigh through my slacks.

Fuck, she's perfect. Somehow, she gets even better at this every fucking time she does it. After five years, she still manages to blow my mind every time she gets her hands or her mouth on me. My little rabbit is insatiable. There aren't many days when she isn't a horny little thing.

Even now, she's dying to fuck. She just had our baby girl a month ago and hasn't been cleared for sex, but she's got her hand down my pants at every available opportunity. Telling her no is impossible, especially since she keeps my fucking dick hard. I live and breathe for this woman.

She rolls my balls between her fingers.

"Goddamn," I growl, my stomach going concave. "I'm going to come."

She hums in delight, greedily taking me deeper. I hit the back of her throat...feel it close around the head of my cock as she swallows. And then I'm thrusting down her throat.

"Ah, fuck!" I shout, delirious with pleasure. I rock my hips, fucking her throat as cum shoots up my shaft. My world goes black, the orgasm blinding me. Blood rushes in my ears in a torrent of sound. All I see is her; all I feel is pleasure.

She swallows every drop I give her, leaving me plastered against the fucking wall and breathing hard. Her proud smile and bright eyes have my dick twitching before he's even fully soft. She wipes beneath her eyes, meeting my gaze.

"Beautiful," I growl, dragging her into my arms to kiss the shit out of her.

She squeals, trying to wiggle free. "You're going to mess up my lipstick!"

"Little one, I already fucked up your lipstick," I mutter against her lips. "Half of it is on my cock right now."

"Darn it," she huffs, elbowing me in the ribs. "I have things to do today."

Of course she does. Nothing slows Catriona down for long. We have three little ones and a brand-new baby, but Catriona never stops. She's full of energy and eager to experience everything life has to offer. After spending so long living under the oppressive thumb of the Vipers, she loves the freedom she has here.

Even though she doesn't need to work, she spends two mornings a week at Gatsby's Books on Main Street. She divides the rest of her time between helping me out at Romano and staying home with the kids. Not that they are home often. Between the playdates, coffee dates, shopping excursions, and other adventures, their days are full. They're at the clubhouse more than I am most weeks.

I fucking love seeing it.

My wife is thriving. Two days after she confronted Connor, Fifth let us know that she wasn't on the radar concerning the investigation. It was a weight off her shoulders. She celebrated by planning a giant Thanksgiving celebration for all my brothers and their families. She said if she was going to be part of our family, she wanted to do it right. The Vipers were spotted in Silver Spoon Falls a few times, but they never got their hands on anyone. They never even got close.

A few weeks later, the feds moved in. By Thanksgiving, they were all in jail. Most of them are still there and will be for a long time. Connor...well, Connor had a few surprises up his sleeve that no one saw coming, Catriona least of all. He was working as an informant to bring the Vipers down. He had been since they started trafficking drugs for the Savages. When Catriona left, he knew it was the best thing for her. The day she went back to confront him, he was trying to protect her the best way he knew how.

Things aren't always what they seem, and people have a way of surprising you. He certainly surprised the fuck out of me. He still did a little time. Far less than anyone else. But Catriona got her brother back. Their relationship is solid.

He and I are a work in progress, and we probably always will be. We've hashed out a lot of shit along the way, but I still don't entirely trust him with her. I may never trust him with her. He did the right thing in the end, but he's still the one who got her into the shit in the first place. She's too goddamn important, and I know exactly how many tears she cried over him. I held her through most of them.

Oddly, he and Giant get along great. He doesn't spend much time around the rest of the MC, though. Like me, they're slow to trust. Especially Cash and Cowboy. It's one thing to hurt us. But when you hurt the women we love, all bets are off. He may have been working as an informant, but Kyra still got hurt. There are no free passes for that bullshit...and second chances are damn hard to come by.

"What are you doing today, rabbit?" I watch as she sets about fixing her lipstick, muttering under her breath about me messing it up...as if I'm the one who took my dick out of my pants and put it in her mouth. Not that I'm going to remind her of that or anything. Are you kidding me? I'm not a complete idiot.

"Stuff," she says.

"What kind of stuff?" I ask, narrowing my eyes in suspicion as I tuck my dick back into my pants.

"Stuff," she says again. "Mind the business that pays you, Andreas Romano."

I pluck her tube of lipstick from her hand and quickly shove the cap back on before tossing it toward my dresser.

"I was using that!" she protests.

"What stuff, Catriona Romano?" I growl, getting up in her personal space. I love my wife beyond all reason. She's the reason my heart beats. I'd fight the armies of heaven and hell for her without hesitation. But she's lost her damn mind if she thinks she's leaving this room without telling me what she's doing today.

I *know* my wife. She's curious and spontaneous and so damn brave. She acts before she thinks and gets in over her head. In short, she's the sole reason I'm going gray. There's not a chance in hell she's leaving this room without fessing up.

"I'm taking dirty pictures on your motorcycle!" she cries.

I blink at her, not sure I heard her correctly. My dick definitely heard her. He's rock hard, thinking about her in nothing but sexy lingerie on the back of my bike. Fuck. Maybe I don't need to work today.

"I hired a photographer and everything," she says, pouting at me. "It was supposed to be a surprise for our anniversary."

"Is the photographer a man or a woman?" I demand.

"Does it matter?"

I narrow my eyes on her.

"You're so ridiculous," she huffs. "I hired a woman, caveman."

"Maybe I should stay home with the kids today," I mutter, pulling her into my arms. "I don't feel well. I could have the flu."

Catriona throws her head back and laughs loudly. "I love you, but you have to leave our house, Andreas. Autumn is coming to watch the kids."

Autumn and her family live in Silver Spoon Falls full-time now and have for the last five years. She had her own journey to take, but it ended with her here. Thank fucking God. My family is home and doing better than ever. My father's ghost no longer haunts us. We've finally put him to rest, picked up the pieces, and moved on.

"I should stay here." I tip my head down to kiss her. "You might need my help. My bike is big and heavy. What if you want to pose outside in the sunlight? I'll need to move it for you."

"Andreas," she laughs against my lips. "The pictures won't be a surprise if you see where I'm posing for them."

"Little one, you'll be half-naked on my motorcycle," I growl, lifting her into my arms. "I'll be hard as a fucking rock and praising God every damn time I see them, surprise or not. I'm staying here. I need this memory to add to my collection."

"You mean your spank bank," she snorts.

"No, the pictures are for the spank bank," I correct, nibbling on her lips. "The memory of you wanting to give me something so fucking perfect is for the collection, rabbit."

"Andreas." She softens in my arms, going pliant, and I know she's done telling me no. When she says my name that like, she usually is.

Collecting new memories of her may be my favorite thing, but making them with me is hers. In that way, we're perfectly matched. In all the ways that matter, we usually are.

"I love you," she whispers.

"I love you too, little one. I always will."

"I know." She smiles at me, those bright eyes full of happiness. And then she laughs quietly and squirms in my arms. "Now put me down, you big jerk. I have to get ready."

"Nah, I think I'll keep you," I growl playfully, stomping toward our bed.

She squeals in protest, but she doesn't fight very hard to get free. Not even when I pin her beneath me to kiss her breathless. Instead, she clings like she always does.

Like she's never going to let me go.

Author's Note

If you enjoyed The Heir, please consider leaving a review! I appreciate them so much!

Are you ready to take a wild ride with the Silver Spoon MC series? The next book in the series, The Rockstar by Loni Ree , releases June 10th!

Next up from me is Easy Surrender.

SILVER SPOON MC

These wealthy Texans have it all—Money, looks, power, their MC, and brothers. The only thing missing is someone to share it all with. There's a shortage of eligible ladies in town but these determined men won't let that slow them down. These MC brothers are going to turn the town of Silver Spoon Falls, Texas, on its ear looking for their curvy soulmates.

Beginning in February 2022, Nichole Rose and Loni Ree are bringing you the Silver Spoon MC Series and these aren't your typical MC romance stories. Nichole and Loni like to keep things light. Come along with us on this wild instalove ride.

The CEO by Loni Ree - February 4, 2022

http://mybook.to/TheCEOLoniRee

The Surgeon by Nichole Rose - March 1, 2022

http://mybook.to/TheSurgeon

The Cowboy by Loni Ree - April 4, 2022 -

https://books2read.com/TheCowboyLoniRee

The Heir by Nichole Rose - May 3, 2022 -

http://mybook.to/TheHeirNR

The Rockstar by Loni Ree - June 10, 2022

https://books2read.com/TheRockstar

The Lawyer by Nichole Rose - July 5, 2022

http://mybook.to/TheLawyerNR

The Architect by Loni Ree- August 5, 2022

books2read.com/TheArchitectLoniRee

The Prodigy by Nichole Rose- September 6, 2022

http://mybook.to/TheProdigyNR

The Prince by Loni Ree - October 7, 2022

https://books2read.com/ThePrinceLoniRee

The Bodyguard by Nichole Rose- November 1, 2022

http://mybook.to/TheBodyguardNR

EASY SURRENDER

This Navy SEAL is ready to wave his white flag of surrender and accept his fate when it comes to his curvy girl.

Beckett "Slate" Jennings

My first mission as a SEAL was almost my last.

Saving Dr. Jane Nayler in Yemen almost destroyed me.

Somehow, I survived and buried that pain deep.

Imagine my surprise when Jane's daughter shows up on my doorstep.

After three years, my neatly ordered world collapses around me.

Constance is everything I never knew I needed—beautiful, curvy, and sweet.

When she looks at me like I'm her hero, I know there's nothing I won't do for her.

Even if it means turning to face the past.

Constance Nayler

I've heard so much about Slate from my mom, I feel like I know him.

When she goes missing overseas, I run right to him.

If anyone can help me, the SEAL who saved her once before can.

She forgot to tell me that he's gorgeous...and bossy as can be.

Every time he looks at me, I feel him in my soul.

When he touches me, I go up in flames.

But time doesn't heal all wounds. It hasn't healed him.

Sometimes, it takes something even stronger.

Lucky for him, my spine was forged from steel.

He might be the hero, but this is one battle I plan to win.

When this possessive Navy SEAL meets the younger curvy girl meant for him, he'll surrender more than his heart to claim her. Get ready to fall hard, fast, and forever for Slate and Constance in this sweet and extra steamy short romance!

Easy Surrender is now available.

WRECKED

One look at his curvy captive and this Mafia boss will risk it all. Even if it means toppling his own kingdom to the ground...

Rafe Valentino

A life in chains was the deal I made with my father to win my twin's freedom.

My soul is black with the things I've done to keep my promise.

I never regretted any of it until now. Until her.

Amalia Santiago's bravado and fierce defiance make me feel alive in a way I never expected.

I was never meant to fall for her.

I don't deserve to put my filthy hands all over her pristine body.

She's supposed to be my prisoner.

But now, she'll become my world instead.

Amalia Santiago

When the devil came for my foster brother, I let him take me in his place.

I swore I'd find a way out of this mess for both of us.

Except Rafe Valentino wasn't supposed to have a heart...

And I wasn't supposed to fall for the ruthless crime boss.

So why do I come alive when he touches me?

Now, I'm one wrong move from destroying everything.

And nothing is what it seems.

How do I sacrifice the man I love to save my brother?

If you enjoy OTT possessive older men with a little bit of darkness in them and sassy, curvy heroines with heart, get ready to fall for Rafe and Amalia in this sweet and extra steamy romance.As always, Nichole Rose books come complete with a guaranteed HEA. Safe read. No cliffhanger. Each book in the Ruined Trilogy features a different Valentino brother and can be read as a standalone story.

Wrecked is now available.

INSTALOVE BOOK CLUB

The Instalove Book Club is now in session!

Get the inside scoop from your favorite instalove authors, meet new authors to love, and snag freebies and bonus content from featured authors every month. The Instalove Book Club newsletter goes out once per week!

Join now to get your hands on bonus scenes and brand-new, exclusive content from our first six featured authors.

Join the Club: http://instaloveinstalovebookclub.com

Follow Nichole

Sign-up for Nichole's mailing list at http://authornichol erose.com/newsletter to stay up to date on all new releases and for exclusive ARC giveaways from Nichole Rose.

Want to connect with Nichole and other readers? Join Nichole Rose's Book Beauties on Facebook!

facebook.com/AuthorNicholeRose/

instagram.com/AuthorNicholeRose

twitter.com/AuthNicholeRose

bookbub.com/authors/nichole-rose

tiktok.com/@authornicholerose

MORE BY NICHOLE ROSE

Her Alpha Series

Her Alpha Daddy Next Door

Her Alpha Boss Undercover

Her Alpha's Secret Baby

Her Alpha Protector

Her Date with an Alpha

Her Alpha: The Complete Series

Her Bride Series

His Future Bride

His Stolen Bride

His Secret Bride

His Curvy Bride

His Captive Bride

His Blushing Bride

His Bride: The Complete Series

Claimed Series
Possessing Liberty
Teaching Rowan
Claiming Caroline
Kissing Kennedy
Claimed: The Complete Series

Love on the Clock Series
Adore You
Hold You
Keep You
Protect You
Love on the Clock: The Complete Series

The Billionaires' Club
The Billionaire's Big Bold Weakness
The Billionaire's Big Bold Wish
The Billionaire's Big Bold Woman
The Billionaire's Big Bold Wonder

Playing for Keeps

Cutie Pie

Ice Breaker

Ice Prince

Ice Giant (coming soon)

The Second Generation

A Blushing Bride for Christmas

Come Undone (currently in Love Always Wins anthology)

Silver Spoon MC

The Surgeon

The Heir

The Lawyer

The Prodigy (coming soon)

The Bodyguard (coming soon)

Echoes of Forever

His Christmas Miracle

Taken by the Hitman

Wicked Saint

The Ruined Trilogy

Physical Science
Wrecked

<u>Destination Romance</u>
Romancing the Cowboy
Beach House Beauty

<u>Standalone Titles</u>
A Touch of Summer
Black Velvet
His Secret Obsession
Dirty Boy
Naughty Little Elf
Devil's Deceit
Wearing Their Pearls

<u>Easy on Me</u>
Easy Ride
Easy Surrender

<u>One Night with You</u>
Falling Hard
Model Behavior

Learning Curve

Angel Kisses

writing with Loni Ree as Loni Nichole

Dillon's Heart (coming soon)

Razor's Flame (coming soon)
Ryker's Reward (coming soon)

Zane's Rebel (coming soon)

About Nichole Rose

Nichole Rose is a short romance author on the west coast. Her books feature headstrong, sassy women and the alpha males who consume them. From grumpy detectives to country boys with attitude to instalove and over-the-top declarations, nothing is off-limits.

Nichole is sure to have a steamy, sweet story just right for everyone. She fully believes the world is ugly enough without trying to fit falling in love into a one-size-fits-all box. When not writing, Nichole enjoys fine wine, cute shoes, and everything supernatural. She is happily married to the love of her life and is a proud mama to the world's most ridiculous fur-babies.

You can learn more about Nichole and her books at authornicholerose.com.

f

facebook.com/AuthorNicholeRose/

instagram.com/AuthorNicholeRose

twitter.com/AuthNicholeRose

bookbub.com/authors/nichole-rose

tiktok.com/@authornicholerose